© 2024 Mojang AB. All Rights Reserved. Minecraft, the Minecraft logo, the Mojang Studios logo and the Creeper logo are trademarks of the Microsoft group of companies.

Published in the United States by Random House Children's Books, a division of Penguin Random House LLC, 1745 Broadway, New York, NY 10019, and in Canada by Penguin Random House Canada Limited, Toronto. Random House and the colophon are registered trademarks of Penguin Random House LLC. First published in Great Britain, in 2023, by HarperCollins UK.

rhcbooks.com
minecraft.net

ISBN 978-0-593-89657-0 (trade)
Printed in the United States of America
10 9 8 7 6 5 4 3 2 1

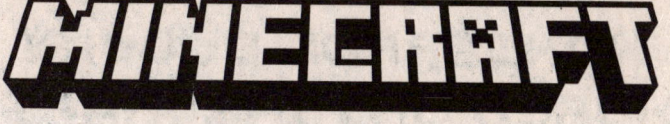

THE OFFICIAL
WOULD YOU
RATHER?

By Thomas McBrien
Illustrated by Joe McLaren

Random House New York

WELCOME TO THE WONDERFUL BLOCKY WORLD OF MINECRAFT!

Steve and Alex have found themselves pondering a series of hilarious, unusual, and challenging situations as they embark on their adventures. Can you help them agree on what to do?

Be warned, though—these decisions won't be easy! With each turn of the page, you will find our heroes in a new scenario, having to choose between two difficult options.

You might find yourself deciding to face the wither without a shield or choosing to have a wandering trader follow you around all day.

Debate with your friends and family to see what options you'd all choose. The answers might surprise you!

ALEX AND STEVE ARE LOOKING FOR THEIR NEXT BIG SURVIVAL ADVENTURE, BUT CAN'T AGREE ON WHICH CHALLENGE THEY SHOULD COMPLETE.

WOULD YOU RATHER . . .

gather every mob for a zoo in an endless thunderstorm

OR

collect every item, but it's always nighttime?

ALEX

Collecting all those items at nighttime would be perilous with hostile mobs around. I vote we collect mobs in a thunderstorm—what's a bit of rain?

STEVE

But gathering every mob for a zoo in a thunderstorm could backfire. Suddenly, there'd be zombified piglins instead of pigs, not to mention charged creepers! At least if we collect the items, we'll have plenty of things to defend ourselves with.

VARIATIONS

WILL THESE VARIATIONS MAKE YOU CHANGE YOUR DECISION?

ENDLESS THUNDERSTORM	ALWAYS NIGHTTIME
■ You have to cart all of your collected mobs around behind you in a long train of minecarts with chests wherever you go.	■ You can only keep one item in your inventory at a time and must bring the rest with you in chests carried by donkeys.
■ You only have two rails for every mob you have, so you are constantly building tracks in order to travel.	■ You are ambushed by hostile mobs while eating a pumpkin and don't have time to get to your donkey for a weapon. On gourd!

9

STEVE AND ALEX NEED A PLACE TO LIVE, BUT DON'T HAVE ENOUGH IN THEIR INVENTORY TO BUILD A NEW BASE. THEY'VE BOTH FOUND EXISTING BASES TO CHOOSE FROM.

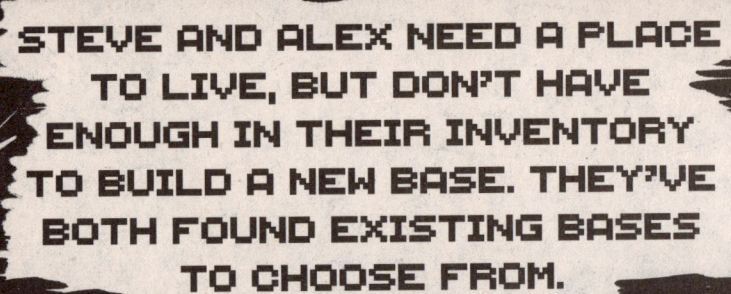

WOULD YOU RATHER...

live in a house made of cobwebs with a resident spider

OR

live in a house made of magma blocks with a resident strider?

STEVE

ALEX

> Bring a warped fungus on a stick and that strider is your new best friend.

> Yeah, as long as you don't step too near the walls! Those hot blocks will leave a mark.

> But living with a spider? You wouldn't be able to sleep with an angry mob nearby.

> Still, I'd rather a hostile mob than a house that wants to attack me! At least the spider can be defeated.

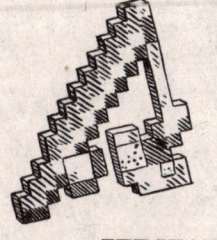

VARIATIONS

SEE IF YOU'D CHANGE YOUR DECISION WITH EACH PAIR OF VARIATIONS BELOW.

A COBWEB HOUSE AND RESIDENT SPIDER	A MAGMA BLOCK HOUSE AND RESIDENT STRIDER
■ The spider invites its friends and family over for a surprise feast: you!	■ You live beneath a *Nether* fortress and are often under attack by blazes.
■ The house slowly fills up with sticky cobwebs that slow you down—but not the spider!	■ The strider insists on having an indoor lava pool right next to your bed.

11

A NEW ADVENTURE AWAITS THESE TWO HEROES: EDUCATION! THERE'S ONLY ENOUGH TICKS IN THE DAY TO MASTER ONE SUBJECT, BUT WHICH DO YOU CHOOSE?

WOULD YOU RATHER...

be able to build incredibly fast   OR   be a redstone genius?

ALEX

Building quickly means growing my world faster. I can finish all my projects and learn more while doing so.

STEVE

With redstone, you can create wonderful and amazing inventions. They could help you do everything you wanted them to!

VARIATIONS

SEE IF YOU'D CHANGE YOUR DECISION WITH EACH PAIR OF VARIATIONS BELOW.

BE ABLE TO BUILD QUICKLY	BE A REDSTONE GENUIS
■ Illagers invade a huge city you built and use it as a base to create an evil empire.	■ Your inventions are stolen by piglin brutes and used as a way to invade the Overworld.
■ You get to invent a new block for the game.	■ You get to add a new redstone item to the game.

13

STEVE HAS FOUND HIMSELF ON THE WRONG SIDE OF THE RIVER. HE DOESN'T WANT TO GET HIS BOOTS WET CROSSING BACK TO HIS BASE, BUT HIS INVENTORY CONTAINS ONLY TWO RESOURCES.

WOULD YOU RATHER...

cross a river on a wide bridge made of ice

OR

cross on a narrow bridge made of honey blocks?

ALEX: The honey blocks will slow you down, but the ice can help you cross it quickly.

STEVE: True, but I have less control over movement and I'm more likely to slip off the ice bridge.

ALEX: Hmm, but the honey block bridge is a lot narrower, so you're more likely to fall anyway.

STEVE: But I can stick to the side of honey blocks if I do fall . . . for a little while at least.

VARIATIONS

SEE IF YOU'D CHANGE YOUR DECISION WITH EACH PAIR OF VARIATIONS BELOW.

WIDE BRIDGE MADE OF ICE	NARROW BRIDGE MADE OF HONEY BLOCKS
■ Someone has set up a campfire beneath the bridge, and the ice is quickly melting.	■ Every fourth honey block is missing, and the honey blocks stop you from jumping.
■ A panda wanders onto the end of the ice bridge. You need it to move to get home, but all you have is a sword.	■ A bee settles on the honey block bridge to eat, and it refuses to move. If you hit it away, its entire hive will attack you.

15

ALEX AND STEVE HAVE BEEN ADVENTURING FOR WEEKS, ONLY TO RETURN HOME AND FIND THAT THEIR FOOD HAS BEEN STOLEN BY FOXES!

WITH ONLY TWO ITEMS LEFT AND LOW HUNGER BARS, THERE'S A DIFFICULT DECISION TO MAKE.

WOULD YOU RATHER...

take your chances eating a feast of poisonous potatoes

OR

pig out on rotten flesh?

STEVE

Ugh, both are gross!

ALEX

Rotten flesh comes from zombies, and some of those zombies used to be villagers! Yuck. Plus, it will probably leave you hungry afterward.

STEVE

Poisonous potatoes are also pretty disgusting, and they could poison you!

VARIATIONS

SEE IF YOU'D CHANGE YOUR DECISION WITH EACH PAIR OF VARIATIONS BELOW.

POISONOUS POTATOES	ROTTEN FLESH
■ The poisonous potatoes give you Slowness but also Invisibility. You are now a mega-slow superhero!	■ The rotten flesh gives you Mining Fatigue but also Strength. Sure, you're hungry and can't mine but watch out hostile mobs!
■ Eat the poisonous potatoes and there's a chance you could become a zombie.	■ Eating the rotten flesh makes you the target of every zombie nearby.

17

STEVE AND ALEX'S BASE IS BESIDE A DROWNED-INFESTED RIVER. BUT AFTER BEING CHASED ACROSS THEIR BRIDGE BY ZOMBIES, THEY'VE BEEN IMAGINING OTHER WAYS TO GET ACROSS.

WOULD YOU RATHER . . .

jump three times as high but lose a health heart

OR

swim twice as fast but only see half the distance?

ALEX

Swimming twice as fast will be super helpful for exploring. If I find a monument, I'll be able to escape the guardians!

 **STEVE**

You might be able to escape the guardians, but you may not spot the monument at all if you can only see half as far.

ALEX

But losing health each time you jump? You won't be able to explore far as you will need to eat all your food.

 **STEVE**

I can bring extra food! I'll be able to jump on top of trees and explore biomes faster.

VARIATIONS

SEE IF YOU'D CHANGE YOUR DECISION WITH EACH PAIR OF VARIATIONS BELOW.

JUMP HIGHER	SWIM FASTER
■ You lose a weapon every time you jump.	■ You lose a piece of armor every time you swim.
■ Every time you jump, there's always a goat ready to ram you when you land.	■ Every time you swim, pufferfish flock to you to puff up.

19

STEVE AND ALEX ARE FISHING AND CHATTING ABOUT WHAT COOL ENCHANTMENTS THEY'D INVENT IF THEY WERE ABLE TO.

WOULD YOU RATHER . . .

have a helmet that allows you to swim in lava   OR   have boots that give you super speed?

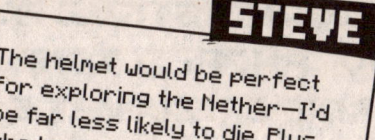

STEVE

The helmet would be perfect for exploring the Nether—I'd be far less likely to die. Plus, who knows what I'd find in the lava lakes!

ALEX

But imagine having super speed! I wouldn't need to spend ages taming an unruly horse to get around quickly.

VARIATIONS

SEE IF YOU'D CHANGE YOUR DECISION WITH EACH PAIR OF VARIATIONS BELOW.

SWIM IN LAVA	SUPER SPEED
■ You can swim in lava but only for 30 seconds before you burst into flames.	■ You are so fast that you can run on water, but only for 30 steps before you sink.
■ The helmet makes everything you look at turn to lava.	■ The boots create ravines wherever you run.

ALEX AND STEVE RUN ACROSS THE OVERWORLD TO ESCAPE FROM A HORDE OF ZOMBIES, BUT THEY ARE NOW TERRIBLY UNPREPARED FOR THEIR NEXT ADVENTURE.

WOULD YOU RATHER...

be stuck in a desert biome with just wood in your inventory

OR

be lost in a deep cave with just food in your inventory?

Caves are dangerous and dark. You will need tools to survive, but without wood, you won't be able to craft any.

ALEX

STEVE

I can search for a mineshaft to collect resources for tools. You may have tools, but what about food? There are mostly undead mobs in the desert!

I can find rabbits for food. Plus, I can defend myself against undead mobs with a wooden sword. How will you keep the mobs at bay without torches?

If you can even catch a rabbit! Those mobs are fast! At least I'll have enough food to last me until I can find a way out of the cave.

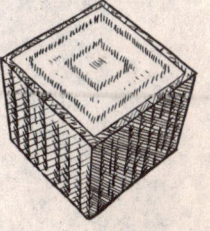

VARIATIONS

SEE IF YOU'D CHANGE YOUR DECISION WITH EACH PAIR OF VARIATIONS BELOW.

DESERT BIOME WITH JUST WOOD	DEEP CAVE WITH JUST FOOD
■ Undead mobs decide to start spreading fire when the sun rises, and one sets your base alight while trying to get inside.	■ You stumble across a cavern full of cobwebs left by a hungry cave spider that is lurking in the darkness, waiting to pounce.
■ A rabbit will show you a quick way out of the desert, but only if you don't eat it or its friends.	■ A friendly bat leads you to the surface, but it takes you the long way!

23

ALEX AND STEVE HAVE MANAGED TO GET THEMSELVES FREE FROM THEIR PREVIOUS PREDICAMENTS . . . ONLY TO FALL STRAIGHT INTO ANOTHER ONE! THEY SHOULD REALLY BE WATCHING WHERE THEY'RE GOING.

WOULD YOU RATHER . . .

be stuck in the snowy plains with only a cookie

OR

be in the deep dark with only one torch?

VARIATIONS

SEE IF YOU'D CHANGE YOUR DECISION WITH EACH PAIR OF VARIATIONS BELOW.

SNOWY PLAINS WITH A COOKIE

- You come across an igloo, but it has a resident zombie villager that isn't good at sharing!

- You can trade your cookie for a golden apple to cure the zombie villager, but you'll lose half your hunger points.

DEEP DARK WITH ONE TORCH

- You find an ancient city full of enough loot to fill your inventory, but there's a warden in your way!

- You can trade your torch for five snowballs to distract the warden, but you'll lose half your health points.

ALEX: The deep dark is scary! One wrong step and I'll summon the warden.

STEVE: Snowy plains are covered by powder snow. One misstep and you'll find yourself crawling through snow or, worse, buried alive!

WOULD YOU RATHER...

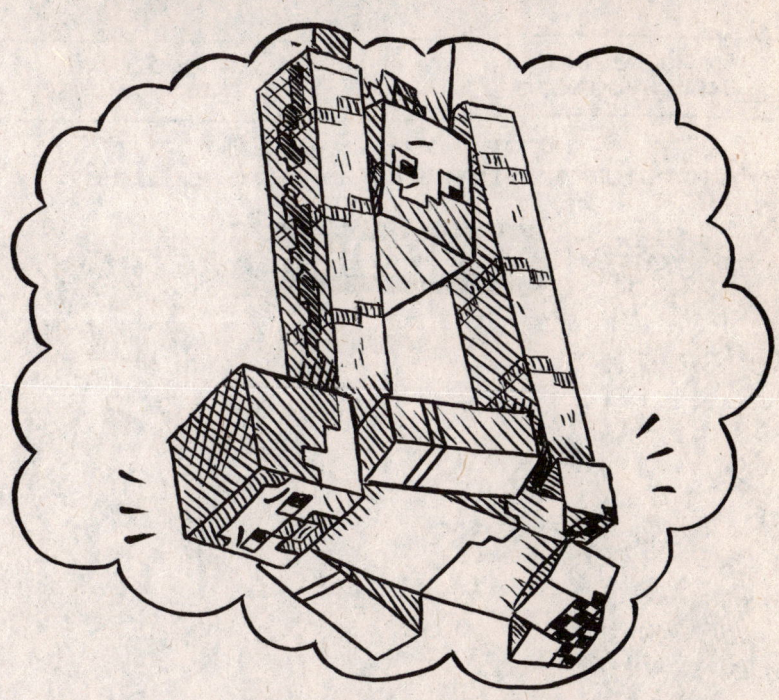

THE SUN HAS SET, AND OUR HEROES ARE HIDING FROM HOSTILE MOBS. IT'S A LONG NIGHT, AND THEY ARE GROWING BORED, SO THEY START AN ODD DEBATE.

wake up with the legs of a creeper

OR

wake up with the arms of an iron golem?

ALEX

Do creepers even have legs?

STEVE

Yes, of course they do. Well, they have feet. That counts! And they're super-stealthy feet, too. I never hear them coming.

I'm not sure we can call the iron golem's arms *arms*. They're more like battering rams.

I'm fairly certain iron golems are so big and strong, they don't even fit through doorways.

VARIATIONS

SEE IF YOU'D CHANGE YOUR DECISION WITH EACH PAIR OF VARIATIONS BELOW.

CREEPER LEGS	IRON GOLEM ARMS
■ You move so quietly that everyone gets startled when they see you, including villagers.	■ You're so strong that all your friends make you do the mining while they do the building.
■ You get so excited when you find diamonds that you sometimes lose control and explode, destroying them.	■ You can't control your strength, so mining basic blocks, such as wood, destroys the block before you can even pick it up.

STEVE HAD A STARTLING
NIGHTMARE. ONE MOMENT HE
WAS FACING ANGRY BABY
ZOMBIES AND THE NEXT HE
WAS BEING CHASED BY A GIANT
SPIDER. NOT KNOWING WHICH
WAS WORSE, HE ASKS ALEX.

WOULD YOU RATHER . . .

fight five baby
zombies at
the same time

OR

be chased by a spider
that's five times the
size and strength of
a usual spider?

STEVE: I can't decide whether five baby zombies running around is worse than one massive spider.

ALEX: Well, those baby zombies are all moving separately. At least the spider is only one thing to keep track of.

Their attacks are not as strong as the spider, though—it would be HUGE! You'd struggle to survive an encounter with one of those.

The spider may hit harder, but the baby zombies move faster. Are you fast enough to avoid them all at once?

VARIATIONS

SEE IF YOU'D CHANGE YOUR DECISION WITH EACH PAIR OF VARIATIONS BELOW.

BABY ZOMBIES	GIANT SPIDER
■ Lightning strikes and something strange happens—the baby zombies now have eight arms, each holding a sword.	■ The spider is bitten by a baby zombie and transforms into a giant zombie spider that can turn you into a zombie, too!
■ The baby zombies find five chickens to ride into battle against you—and they peck!	■ The spider is hit with a splash potion of Swiftness, and now it's twice as fast.

THE SUN IS RISING, AND
ALEX AND STEVE HAVE
ALMOST SURVIVED THE
NIGHT. IT'S NOT QUITE
SAFE TO GO OUTSIDE
YET, SO THEY DECIDE TO
HAVE A DEBATE ABOUT
SURVIVAL CHALLENGES.

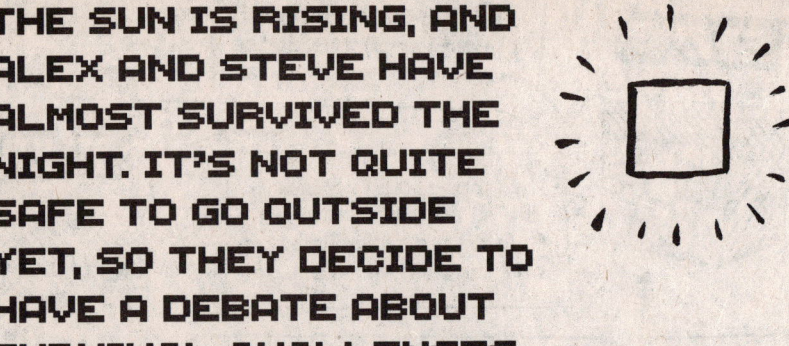

WOULD YOU RATHER . . .

be able to explore
the entire
Overworld, but it's
always nighttime

OR

be stuck on a tiny
island where it's
always daytime?

30

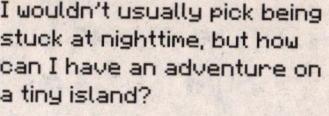

I wouldn't usually pick being stuck at nighttime, but how can I have an adventure on a tiny island?

ALEX

STEVE

There's the entire ocean around that island! Don't forget that hostile mobs come out at nighttime.

Drowned can spawn underwater at any time of day. That ocean will be riddled with them hiding in the depths!

Yes, but at least they can't step out of the water without burning. The Overworld will be swarming with mobs in constant nighttime.

VARIATIONS

SEE IF YOU'D CHANGE YOUR DECISION WITH EACH PAIR OF VARIATIONS BELOW.

NIGHTTIME OVERWORLD	DAYTIME ISLAND
■ Mobs keep on flocking to your base, and if you stay still for too long, you risk an army gathering outside your walls.	■ Before long, your island is surrounded by drowned lurking beneath the ocean, just waiting for you to run out of food.
■ You find a village guarded by iron golems and well lit against the nighttime by plenty of torches.	■ A dolphin comes along and offers to help you find buried treasure in return for some raw fish.

31

ALEX AND STEVE HAVE GATHERED A BUNCH OF NOTE BLOCKS TOGETHER TO CREATE A TUNE, BUT CAN'T DECIDE WHAT THEY WANT THEM TO PLAY.

WOULD YOU RATHER . . .

play for five hours with heavy metal music playing super slowly

OR

play for five hours with opera music playing mega fast?

ALEX

Even slowed down, I think heavy metal music would really get me in the mood for mining.

STEVE

Sure, but for five hours? If it's super slow, those five hours will feel super long! Opera music sped up would make the time fly past and really get me in the mood for exploring the Overworld.

ALEX

But opera music mega fast would be really intense! Heavy metal music slowed down would be almost relaxing. . . .

STEVE

Hmm, I'm not sure it would. Intense suits me. I like to live life in the fast lane!

VARIATIONS

SEE IF YOU'D CHANGE YOUR DECISION WITH EACH PAIR OF VARIATIONS BELOW.

SLOW HEAVY METAL	FAST OPERA
■ The heavy metal music is sung by screaming goats.	■ The opera music is sung by villagers.
■ The screaming goats follow you around, ramming you in time with the beat.	■ The singing villagers wander after you, constantly getting in your way.

IT'S TIME FOR THE GREAT MINECRAFT RACE OFF! ALEX AND STEVE HAVE MADE IT TO THE FINAL ROUND AND ARE ABOUT TO DISCOVER WHICH MOB THEY'LL HAVE TO FIND AND BRING BACK.

WOULD YOU RATHER...

have to retrieve a brown mooshroom   OR   bring back a lazy panda?

ALEX

Our best bet of finding mooshrooms is on a mushroom fields island. You can search an entire ocean before finding one of those.

STEVE

Yes, but once I find the island, I'm all set! Lazy pandas are not easy to find. Finding a panda is already hard, and then you'll need to find a lazy one!

ALEX

Not if all the mooshrooms are red when you get there! I'm not worried about finding the pandas. Jungle biomes can be seen from far away because the trees are so tall.

STEVE

Red mooshrooms can be turned brown. I'll just need some lightning and a lot of luck! You can't change the personality of a panda if you find a different kind.

VARIATIONS

SEE IF YOU'D CHANGE YOUR DECISION WITH EACH PAIR OF VARIATIONS BELOW.

BROWN MOOSHROOM	LAZY PANDA
■ You can only find red mooshrooms, and you forgot to pack wheat to breed a brown one.	■ The lazy panda you find has no interest in following you quickly. You'll have to drag it back to win.
■ When seeking lightning to turn your red mooshroom brown, a pig is also struck. Argh! A zombified piglin!	■ The panda gets distracted by a nearby pillager birthday party and leaves you to go eat their cake.

35

STEVE AND ALEX LOVE NOTHING MORE THAN DISCOVERING A NEW MOB IN MINECRAFT. THEY OFTEN WONDER WHAT THEY MIGHT LIKE TO UNCOVER NEXT.

WOULD YOU RATHER . . .

discover a super-cute mob that constantly trips you up

OR

find a super-creepy mob that sings you catchy songs?

STEVE

ALEX

I can't resist a cute mob.

A cute mob that will follow you around, tripping you up? You'll never get anything done!

But a creepy, singing mob? As soon as it starts, I'll have silly song lyrics stuck in my head all day.

Just because they're catchy songs doesn't mean that they're bad songs!

VARIATIONS

SEE IF YOU'D CHANGE YOUR DECISION WITH EACH PAIR OF VARIATIONS BELOW.

CUTE MOB	CREEPY MOB
■ The cute mob loves to dance and insists on doing it all day long, knocking over everything in its path, including all your things.	■ The creepy mob teaches villagers how to sing the songs, too. They practice outside your base every morning. It sounds bad!
■ The cute mob opens the door to absolutely everyone—including any zombies that come knocking at night!	■ The creepy mob tries to sing you to sleep, but it has the opposite effect—now phantoms are here!

37

ALEX HAS SPENT THE NIGHT
TOSSING AND TURNING. SHE HAD A
NIGHTMARE ABOUT BEING CHASED
BY PIGLINS AND REACHING THE
SAFTEY OF A VILLAGE, ONLY TO BE
TURNED AWAY. SHE DECIDES TO ASK
STEVE WHAT HE WOULD PREFER.

WOULD YOU RATHER . . .

be barred from
every village

OR

be disliked by
every piglin?

ALEX

I spend too much time in the Nether to have every piglin angry with me. I always wear my golden helmet to show them I'm friendly.

STEVE

You would rather be prevented from entering villages? They're the sanctuaries of the Overworld. When you see a village, you know there's an iron golem to keep you safe while you sleep.

ALEX

Bah, I don't need any help from iron golems! I'd rather barter for fire charges, Ender pearls, and potions of Fire Resistance from piglins.

STEVE

Piglin trades are useful, but are they as useful as villagers' trades? Villagers can sell me almost anything I could ever want.

VARIATIONS

SEE IF YOU'D CHANGE YOUR DECISION WITH EACH PAIR OF VARIATIONS BELOW.

BARRED FROM VILLAGES	DISLIKED BY PIGLINS
■ All villagers and iron golems chase you on sight, so you can never get near a village again.	■ Piglins hunt you down whenever you step foot in the Nether.
■ All piglins love you, including piglin brutes, and you even have a pet hoglin called Holly.	■ You have your own iron golem companion called Ivor that gives you a poppy every day.

39

OUR HEROES HAVE ADVENTURED FAR AND WIDE TO FIND THE PERFECT LOCATION FOR THEIR NEW BASE. NOW THAT THEY HAVE, ALEX WANTS TO FOCUS ON BUILDING FARMS FOR FOOD, WHILE STEVE WANTS TO BEFRIEND THE NEARBY VILLAGERS.

WOULD YOU RATHER . . .

have all the semiautomatic farms you need

OR

have unlimited villager trades?

ALEX

Farms will provide us with all the food we need in the coming weeks.

STEVE

Villagers can trade lots of super-useful tools and equipment. They can save us hours in resource gathering.

You will still need resources to trade with the villagers. With crops, we can stay fed.

With unlimited trades, we could have stacks and stacks of emeralds in no time. Then we can get ourselves some shiny diamond armor for adventuring.

VARIATIONS

SEE IF YOU'D CHANGE YOUR DECISION WITH EACH PAIR OF VARIATIONS BELOW.

SEMIAUTOMATIC FARMS	UNLIMITED TRADES
■ Your semiautomatic farms provide you with all the crops you need to survive, but you can't trade them with villagers.	■ The villagers love you and offer you half price on everything, but you have to grow crops one at a time.
■ The farms attract mobs from all around. Every day, one of your fields is overrun by a swarm of angry bees.	■ The success of the village has attracted hostile wolves. They scare away the villagers unless you stop them.

41

TRAVELING
DEEPER AND
DEEPER INTO
THE WILDERNESS,
STEVE AND ALEX
HAVE STARTED
TO NOTICE SOME
PECULIAR BEHAVIOR
AMONG THE LOCAL MOBS.

WOULD YOU RATHER ...

play in a plains biome plagued by pesky crop-stealing sheep

OR

spawn in a taiga biome filled with annoying emerald-stealing foxes?

STEVE

There are sheep everywhere in the plains biome. We'll never be able to have a farm if they eat all the crops!

ALEX

I can build a fence around the crops to stop the sheep from eating them. Keeping your emeralds safe from foxes will be harder—those sly mobs can sneak in anywhere.

I'm not worried about the foxes. How many could there really be?

In a taiga biome? Who knows. They're always spawning there.

VARIATIONS

SEE IF YOU'D CHANGE YOUR DECISION WITH EACH PAIR OF VARIATIONS BELOW.

CROP-STEALING SHEEP	EMERALD-STEALING FOXES
■ Baby sheep are super nimble and can climb over fences into any garden and open any gate. There's no keeping them out!	■ The foxes are organized and arrange heists to steal as many emeralds as they can carry every night.
■ Any sheep that don't manage to steal your crops will steal a block from your base instead.	■ Foxes that fail in stealing an emerald will set fire to wooden structures.

43

TWO UNFRIENDLY MOBS HAVE ENTERED ALEX AND STEVE'S CAMP. THEY WON'T LEAVE OUR HEROES ALONE, SO EACH OF THEM MUST TAKE CARE OF ONE OF THE MOBS.

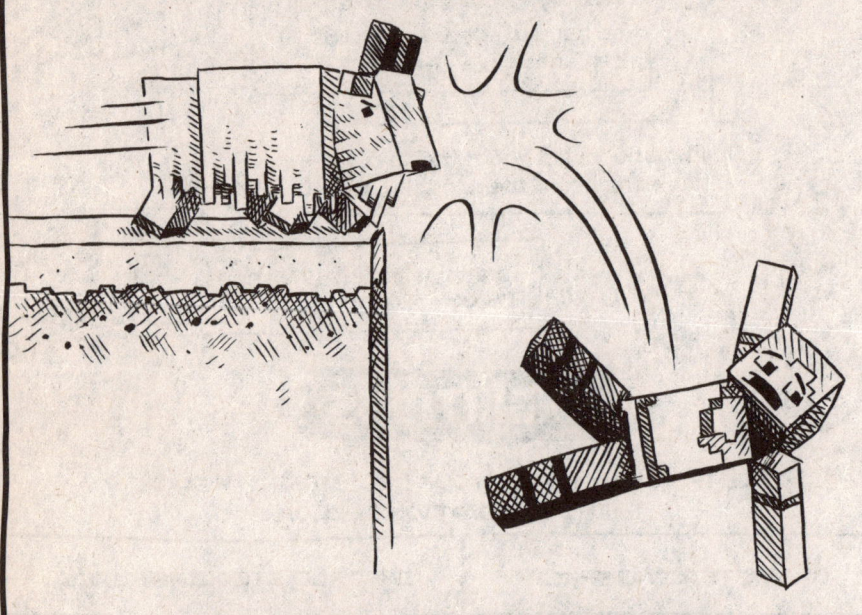

WOULD YOU RATHER . . .

be followed around by a goat that rams you every time you stop

OR

be accompanied by a snow golem that provokes mobs to attack you?

STEVE

A cute goat? Yes, please! My pets always get lost, but this one will be close by whenever I stop.

ALEX

Yes, but it will also ram you every time. That would get super annoying! The snow golem could be useful—its snowballs will be refreshing in the desert.

Its snowballs won't do you any good against all the mobs it provokes and sends your way!

Pfft, I can take them. Besides, you're no safer with the goat—you're at risk of it knocking you off mountain tops if you stop to take in the view!

VARIATIONS

SEE IF YOU'D CHANGE YOUR DECISION WITH EACH PAIR OF VARIATIONS BELOW.

GOAT	SNOW GOLEM
■ The goat dislikes barriers and kicks down any blocks you place that are not a part of your base.	■ The snow golem throws snowballs at you whenever you try to build.
■ The goat has nightmares and screams all night. Its bleating attracts nearby hostile mobs to your base.	■ The snow golem is scared of the dark and doesn't let you sleep. After three nights, phantoms start spawning.

45

OUR HEROES ARE BACK ON THE MOVE! HOWEVER, THEY HAVE GATHERED SO MANY ITEMS IN THEIR BASE, THEY HAVE NO OPTION BUT TO BRING A CHEST WITH THEM!

WOULD YOU RATHER . . .

be stuck riding a
mule with a chest   OR   be trapped on a
in the Nether   boat with a chest
                           in the Overworld?

STEVE: Easy. I'd go on a mule with a chest. Mules can get across all terrains, so there's no need to worry about detours.

ALEX: I'm not so sure. If the mule falls into the lava, all the items in the chest will be destroyed by the fire. At least with a boat, you can always sail around.

You can't sail the boat on land, though. You'll be stuck traveling around the coastline!

There is a lot to see on the coastline. And I can travel up rivers to reach farther inland.

VARIATIONS

SEE IF YOU'D CHANGE YOUR DECISION WITH EACH PAIR OF VARIATIONS BELOW.

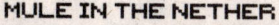

MULE IN THE NETHER	BOAT IN THE OVERWORLD
■ Your mule runs away from hoglins. You'll have to get creative if you're going to keep your food stores full.	■ There's a gang of drowned waiting to pull you under if you ever stop anywhere for more than 30 seconds.
■ You strike up a friendship with a piglin, who will trade with you for any items you need.	■ You have an allay companion that collects any items you ask it to.

47

ALEX AND STEVE DON'T HAVE A MOB TO RIDE AS THEY TREK ACROSS THE OVERWORLD, SO THEY START TO DAYDREAM ABOUT FLYING.

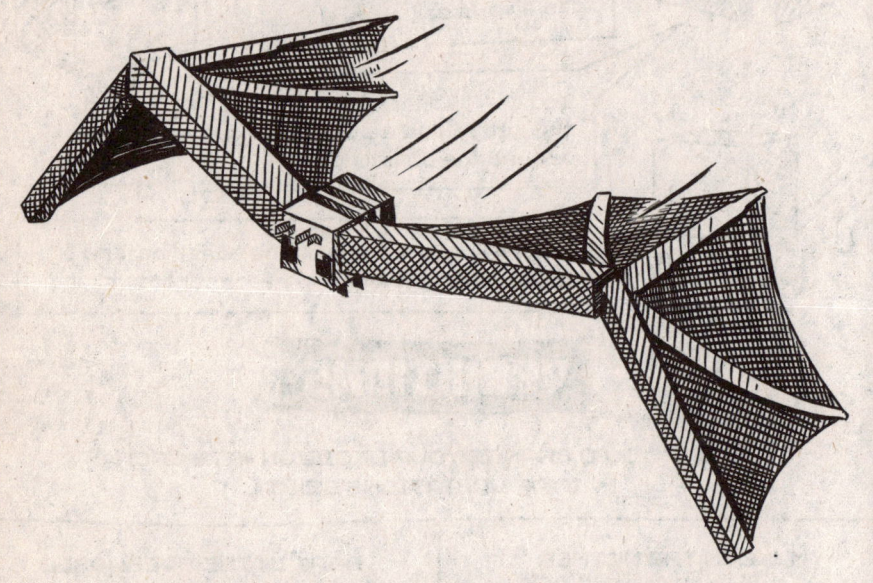

WOULD YOU RATHER . . .

be an Ender Dragon with the wings of a bee

OR

be a bee with the wings of an Ender Dragon?

The Ender Dragon is mighty and fearsome because of its size—you couldn't lose its body.

 STEVE

 ALEX

But would bee wings even carry an Ender Dragon's body? The nimble bee's body with large wings will give you much more mobility.

But a bee would look ridiculous with Ender Dragon wings! With the Ender Dragon's body, I can breathe fire all over the ground to defeat any hostile mobs that come close.

No more ridiculous than a huge dragon with tiny bee wings! At least as a bee, I can make honey!

VARIATIONS

SEE IF YOU'D CHANGE YOUR DECISION WITH EACH PAIR OF VARIATIONS BELOW.

ENDER DRAGON BODY	BEE BODY
■ You are stuck in the End with players constantly attacking you.	■ People keep on stealing your honey, but if you strike back, you'll lose your stinger.
■ Your wings are too small to carry your gigantic dragon body for more than ten seconds at a time.	■ Your wings are so large in comparison to your tiny bee body that you can't control which direction you fly in.

49

OUR ADVENTURERS HAVE FOUND A MAP AND ARE NOW OFF SEARCHING FOR TREASURE. HOWEVER, THEY'RE SO DISTRACTED FOLLOWING THEIR COMPASSES THAT THEY ACCIDENTALLY STUMBLE INTO ANOTHER TRICKY SITUATION.

WOULD YOU RATHER...

find yourself dropped into a dungeon full of zombies with just a wooden sword

OR

get lost in a deep, abandoned mine with just a wooden pickaxe?

STEVE

There's a chance that the abandoned mine contains useful items to scavenge: rails, torches, even diamonds.

ALEX

That is true, but there's definitely a treasure chest in that dungeon. I could be rewarded with enchanted items or gold ingots!

Treasure is only useful if you can bring it home. That wooden sword will make slow work of dealing with the zombies.

How many zombies can there be? A wooden pickaxe won't last you long in a mine—and you wouldn't even be able to collect gold, emeralds, or diamonds with it!

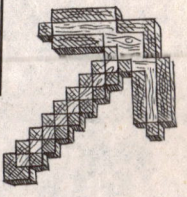

VARIATIONS

SEE IF YOU'D CHANGE YOUR DECISION WITH EACH PAIR OF VARIATIONS BELOW.

DUNGEON WITH WOODEN SWORD	MINE WITH WOODEN PICKAXE
■ The roomful of zombies are now accompanied by baby zombies, and the lights are off!	■ Your wooden pickaxe is well on its way to breaking, and now you've run out of food!
■ Inside the treasure chest is an item you've been searching for, but taking it causes twice as many zombies to spawn.	■ You find a powered minecart track, but you don't know which way to go—one way will lead you out and the other into lava!

51

STEVE IS PLANNING TO SEARCH FOR TREASURE IN AN ANCIENT CITY. ALEX DARES HIM TO MAKE HIS ADVENTURE MORE INTERESTING BY LIMITING HIS INVENTORY.

WOULD YOU RATHER . . .

explore an ancient city with just two blocks of wool

OR

explore the city with just ten snowballs?

Ancient cities are where wardens live. They're blind but will detect even the smallest of movements. Throwing a snowball could distract one in a sticky situation.

ALEX

STEVE

It's not safe to collect the snowballs after throwing them. If I'm not careful, I may run out before I even reach the treasure!

Two blocks of wool could be risky. You'd have to mine them as you move. Plus, if you walk on the edge of the block, there's a chance the sculk sensor will still detect it!

Still, at least there's a better chance of not having to face the warden at all!

VARIATIONS

SEE IF YOU'D CHANGE YOUR DECISION WITH EACH PAIR OF VARIATIONS BELOW.

TWO WOOL BLOCKS	TEN SNOWBALLS
■ It takes so long to move with just the two wool blocks that your hunger points are getting dangerously low.	■ Stumbling around in the dark, you trigger multiple sculk sensors. Now there are five wardens hunting you down!
■ You keep on falling off your wool blocks and triggering sculk sensors. Before you know it, you're faced with a warden!	■ After throwing five snowballs, the wardens figure out that they're being duped. You now have to be clever with your final throws.

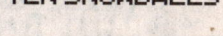

ALEX AND STEVE ARE OUT EXPLORING A BEACH BIOME WHEN THEY'RE PRESENTED WITH TWO NEW OPPORTUNITIES FOR ADVENTURE. WHICH OPTION SHOULD THEY CHOOSE?

WOULD YOU RATHER . . .

follow a dolphin that leads you to a treasure chest defended by hordes of drowned

OR

have an explorer map that leads you to a woodland mansion guarded by pillagers?

STEVE

There's a chance the dolphin will show us to a treasure chest containing another explorer map. Think of the adventure we'd have!

Woodland mansions can provide you with much more than a treasure chest. They contain rare items!

ALEX

Good luck surviving a woodland mansion—it will also be guarded by evokers and vindicators! I might find a heart of the sea in a treasure chest.

Treasure chests are not so easily found. Even with a dolphin to help, you could still spend days digging around in the sand before you find it, while also fending off loads of drowned!

VARIATIONS

SEE IF YOU'D CHANGE YOUR DECISION WITH EACH PAIR OF VARIATIONS BELOW.

TREASURE CHEST	WOODLAND MANSION
■ Every drowned is armed with a trident and ready to throw it at you.	■ Upon entering the woodland mansion, a gaggle of evokers launch vexes at you.
■ A group of angry, but seriously adorable, axolotls swarm the drowned, distracting them from the treasure for two minutes.	■ You liberate a bunch of allays from the structure, that then fly off to retrieve treasure for you!

55

STEVE AND ALEX IMAGINE THAT THEY HAVE BEEN CAPTURED BY A CRAFTY EVOKER THAT GIVES THEM TWO OPTIONS FOR ESCAPE. BUT WHICH ONE SHOULD THEY CHOOSE?

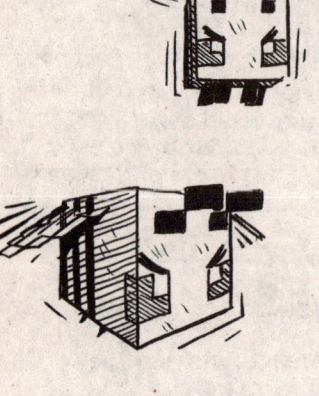

WOULD YOU RATHER . . .

fight a creeper with a flint and steel

OR

fend off ten angry bees with a hoe?

STEVE

I vote we take our chances with the bees! Surely ten bees can't do as much damage as an exploding creeper!

ALEX

But with the flint and steel, we could force the creeper to ignite and run past it before it explodes.

I don't know. . . .That's mighty risky if you ask me. What if you weren't fast enough? The hoe's extra range will help keep the bees off you.

But bees move quickly. And even if you managed to defeat a few, there's more of them to contend with!

VARIATIONS

SEE IF YOU'D CHANGE YOUR DECISION WITH EACH PAIR OF VARIATIONS BELOW.

CREEPER WITH FLINT AND STEEL	ANGRY BEES WITH HOE
■ Exploding the creeper alerts pillagers of your escape, and they're now swarming up the stairs.	■ You swing with your hoe and miss a bee instead battering a bee nest. Now you have three more bees after you!
■ You run into a room filled with TNT. Your creeper escape just got a lot more interesting!	■ You run into a room filled with bee nests—one wrong move and you'll unleash yet another hive!

57

STEVE IS WRITING A TALE TO TEACH BABY VILLAGERS WHY THEY SHOULDN'T GO OUT ALONE INTO THE WILD. ALL HE HAS LEFT TO DO IS DECIDE HOW THE FINAL BOSS BATTLE WILL GO.

WOULD YOU RATHER...

face a charged creeper while wearing a full set of iron armor

OR

be chased by a regular creeper while wearing just diamond leggings for armor!

VARIATIONS

SEE IF YOU'D CHANGE YOUR DECISION WITH EACH PAIR OF VARIATIONS BELOW.

IRON ARMOR	DIAMOND LEGGINGS
■ The charged creeper has followed you to a cave. You're being chased down a narrow tunnel.	■ You're in a forest and get caught in low-hanging leaves. You can't escape the creeper easily.
■ The only way to escape the charged creeper is to lose it in the dark, but you're surrounded by sculk sensors.	■ You jump into a ravine to escape the creeper, but you don't have enough equipment to climb back up.

ALEX AND STEVE HAVE JUST RETURNED FROM SEPARATE ADVENTURES, HAVING FACED FORMIDABLE MOBS. BOTH BRAG THAT THEIR ORDEAL WAS WORSE AND GET A LITTLE CARRIED AWAY.

WOULD YOU RATHER . . .

wake up to find the sky outside full of hungry Ender Dragons

OR

get up to discover someone has just spawned a bunch of withers inside your base?

ALEX

Withers are the worst! They completely destroyed my base when they exploded! At least you could lead the Ender Dragons away from your base.

STEVE

I was lucky to survive all those Ender Dragons outside! At least there's a chance your base would hold the withers long enough for you to escape!

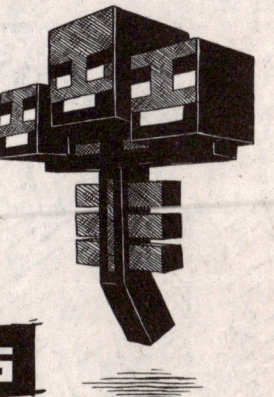

VARIATIONS

SEE IF YOU'D CHANGE YOUR DECISION WITH EACH PAIR OF VARIATIONS BELOW.

ENDER DRAGONS	WITHERS
■ Thankfully, you happened to go to sleep in a full set of diamond armor.	■ It just so happens that you have a potion of Strength in your inventory.
■ The Ender Dragons invite you to their street party, complete with an all-you-can-eat villager buffet.	■ The withers throw you a housewarming party and invite all your friends along—it's a real blast!

ALEX AND STEVE HAVE FOUND THEMSELVES AT THE EDGE OF TWO BIOMES AND AREN'T SURE WHICH ONE TO CHOOSE FOR THEIR NEXT ADVENTURE.

WOULD YOU RATHER . . .

go mining in a snowy mountains biome

OR

search for treasure in a desert biome?

STEVE

Snowy slopes are rich in emerald ore. They're a great place to go mining.

Getting to the top is a big climb, though. The desert is flat, so you can see a pyramid from far away!

ALEX

Deserts are haunted by husks, which are basically zombies that survive in the daylight. They sound terrible!

True, but there are no generated structures in the snowy mountains and plenty of strays outside! Pyramid chests can contain useful items, such as saddles. That's worth fighting a few husks for!

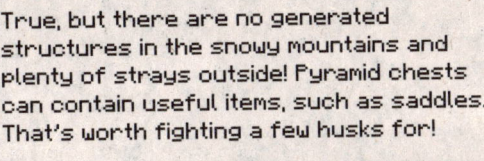

VARIATIONS

SEE IF YOU'D CHANGE YOUR DECISION WITH EACH PAIR OF VARIATIONS BELOW.

SNOWY MOUNTAINS	DESERT BIOME
▪ You find heaps of emeralds underground, but you've now used all your equipment and can't dig your way back out.	▪ You find a desert pyramid that contains all the loot of your dreams, but you didn't pack enough food for the return trip.
▪ You finally see a way out up ahead. Wait, what just hit you? That was a tipped arrow! The way out is guarded by strays, and you are now inflicted with Slowness.	▪ You are set upon by a group of husks. You survive the attack but are hit with Hunger. On the bright side, you now have enough food, but it's all rotting flesh.

63

ALEX AND STEVE HAVE BEEN SHARING STORIES ABOUT PAST ADVENTURES. BOTH THINK THAT THEIRS WOULD BE THE WORST TO RELIVE. CAN YOU HELP SETTLE THEIR DEBATE?

WOULD YOU RATHER...

be caught up in a village raid

OR

find yourself in an unprotected village during a nighttime thunderstorm?

Thunderstorms are dangerous. Lightning can strike half your health bar in one hit.

ALEX

STEVE

But the only warning you have of an incoming raid is the ringing of the town bell.

Lightning can transform mobs, though. Villagers become witches, and pigs become zombified piglins. And let's hope no creepers become charged!

Village raids last up to eight waves, and each one has more difficult mobs than the last. You might even have to defeat ravagers and evokers!

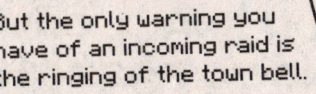

VARIATIONS

SEE IF YOU'D CHANGE YOUR DECISION WITH EACH PAIR OF VARIATIONS BELOW.

VILLAGE RAID	NIGHTTIME THUNDERSTORM
■ Just when you've survived the village raid, another player with the Bad Omen status effect comes along, triggering *another* raid!	■ The sky thunders, and lightning strikes a horde of creepers. Four skeleton horsemen and four charged creepers appear.
■ When trying to defeat a pillager, you accidentally hit an iron golem instead, turning it hostile. Now it's chasing after you while you're still battling the mobs from the raid.	■ The storm is over, and you managed to survive. But many of the villagers were hit by lightning, and now the village is full of witches.

65

ALEX AND STEVE TAKE SHELTER FOR THE NIGHT INSIDE A SMALL CAVE. WITH NOTHING TO PASS THE TIME, THEY START A STRANGE DEBATE ABOUT MOBS.

WOULD YOU RATHER . . .

have zombies as allies, but chickens throw rotten eggs at you

OR

have pillagers for friends, but pigs fart at you?

Having zombie allies at night would be mighty useful—that's far fewer mobs attacking us. Besides, I wouldn't want a pig farting at me!

ALEX

But think of all the pillager outposts we could visit if they were our friends. Being hit with a rotten egg sounds horrendous!

STEVE

VARIATIONS

SEE IF YOU'D CHANGE YOUR DECISION WITH EACH PAIR OF VARIATIONS BELOW.

ZOMBIE ALLIES	PILLAGER FRIENDS
■ If you are hit by a rotten egg, you will be inflicted with the Weakness status effect.	■ If a pig farts within six blocks of you, you'll be inflicted with the Nausea status effect.
■ A baby zombie thinks you're its parent and valiantly fights off mobs for you as long as you tuck it into bed at the end of the night.	■ A pillager falls in love with you and brings you an item every morning to win your affections, but they won't leave you alone.

HALFWAY THROUGH THE NIGHT, ALEX AND STEVE REALIZE THAT THEIR HEALTH IS LOW AND THEIR RESOURCES ARE EMPTY. WITHOUT ANY AMENITIES IN THEIR TINY CAVE, THEY DISTRACT THEMSELVES WITH A DEBATE.

WOULD YOU RATHER...

not be able to drink until you find a spawned pink sheep

OR

not be able to eat until you discover a brown panda?

ALEX: I vote we search for the pink sheep. Brown pandas are super rare, and I'll get peckish!

STEVE: Pink sheep aren't common, either. What if you need to drink before we found one? You can survive longer without food than water!

VARIATIONS

SEE IF YOU'D CHANGE YOUR DECISION WITH EACH PAIR OF VARIATIONS BELOW.

PINK SHEEP	BROWN PANDA
■ Wherever you travel, you are never out of earshot of a flowing waterfall. This makes you super thirsty, but you can't drink from it!	■ While you search for the panda, a villager follows you around, constantly baking fresh cookies. It's all you can smell!
■ You can't hear any mobs approaching over the sound of waterfalls, so they keep sneaking up on you.	■ The villager invents a song about cookies that is not only super annoying but provokes nearby mobs.

ALEX AND STEVE
WANT TO SEARCH FOR
SOMEWHERE NEW TO
EXPLORE. HOWEVER,
NEWS REPORTS OF
ROAMING ILLAGERS
HAVE THEM WORRIED.
THEY CANNOT LEAVE
THEIR BELOVED
MOBS BEHIND.

WOULD YOU RATHER...

lead a group of
goats across
a jagged
mountain biome

OR

lead a horse
through a
jungle filled
with rivers?

Goats can be challenging mobs to herd, but they're also excellent climbers. A journey across the mountain may not be so difficult.

ALEX

STEVE

As long as you're careful where you step. Those jagged peaks have a lot of precarious ledges. You won't be able to turn away from the goats or they may send you flying!

The jungle route may not be so dangerous, but it will take time. There are many low-hanging branches that will force you to dismount.

Crossing over the rivers won't be easy, either. We don't have a boat for the horse to get across.

VARIATIONS

SEE IF YOU'D CHANGE YOUR DECISION WITH EACH PAIR OF VARIATIONS BELOW.

GOATS THROUGH MOUNTAINS	A HORSE THROUGH JUNGLES AND RIVERS
■ One of your herd is a screaming goat and tries to ram you off the edge of the mountain whenever you turn your back.	■ The horse is scared of water and refuses to go near it. To travel anywhere, you must build bridges across every river.
■ The goat continues to scream through the night, and the rest of the herd starts bleating, attracting every nearby mob to your location.	■ All of those bridges make a clear path for every mob in the jungle to follow you at night, giving you no way to escape.

ALEX AND STEVE ARE PLANNING
ON INFILTRATING A BASTION
REMNANT AND THEN SNEAKING
IN TO TRADE IN A VILLAGE THEY
PREVIOUSLY UPSET. TO FIT IN,
THEY'RE GOING TO NEED THE
BEST DISGUISES. BUT WHAT IF
THEY GET STUCK THAT WAY?

WOULD YOU RATHER...

get trapped
looking like   OR   be stuck
a piglin   talking like
                          a villager?

Those piglin outfits don't look very comfortable. Talking like a villager would be fun—maybe I'd be able to understand all the villagers.

ALEX

But only villagers would be able to understand you. We wouldn't be able to understand each other anymore. Think how easy it would be to loot a bastion remnant disguised as a piglin!

STEVE

We'd just have to communicate through emotes or signs! If you were stuck looking like a piglin, you'd never be accepted in a village again—iron golems would attack you on sight!

VARIATIONS

SEE IF YOU'D CHANGE YOUR DECISION WITH EACH PAIR OF VARIATIONS BELOW.

LOOK LIKE A PIGLIN	TALK LIKE A VILLAGER
■ You are accepted into a piglin group, but to pass the initiation, you must first hunt a hoglin for dinner!	■ The villagers accept you as one of their own and even give you robes to fit your profession. Congrats, you are now a nitwit!
■ To stay undercover, you embrace the piglins' obsession with gold, even allowing your piglin friends to dig up your house in search of it.	■ You struggle to get to sleep, so you wander around restlessly at night attracting a zombie siege that threatens to overcome the village.

73

ALEX IS THINKING TO HERSELF ABOUT THE WORST POSSIBLE PLACE TO SPAWN. OF COURSE, THAT DEPENDS ON WHO AND WHAT YOU ARE!

WOULD YOU RATHER...

be an Enderman spawning in the ocean

OR

be a skeleton spawning in the desert sun?

74

Endermen hate the water and teleport each time they touch it! If they're in an ocean, they'll keep teleporting and taking damage all day and all night until they find land!

Skeletons are undead. They'll catch fire in the sun. There isn't much shade in the desert, so the chances of you lasting until nightfall is slim.

VARIATIONS

SEE IF YOU'D CHANGE YOUR DECISION WITH EACH PAIR OF VARIATIONS BELOW.

ENDERMAN IN OCEAN	SKELETON IN DESERT
■ The Enderman has a special pair of swimming trunks that saves it from water damage but gives it a wedgie that slows it down.	■ The skeleton wraps itself from head to toe in toilet paper to avoid burning up in the sun, but this often trips it up.
■ The Enderman becomes a drowned Enderman. It searches for underwater structures to grief.	■ The skeleton becomes a mummy, a new mob that prevents players from sleeping in deserts.

75

STEVE HAS FINISHED
BUILDING HIS EMERGENCY
SHELTER FOR THE EVENING.
HE REALLY WISHES
THE NIGHT WASN'T
SO TERRIFYING. HE
WONDERS IF LIFE
IS ANY EASIER FOR
SOME OF THE MOBS
OUTSIDE.

WOULD YOU RATHER . . .

be a zombie
that's afraid   OR
of the dark

a drowned
that's afraid
of fish?

Zombies live in the dark. They can't step into the sun without burning.

True! But they can live in a lit cave. Drowned spend all day under the sea, surrounded by fish!

But they could get out at night to escape the fish. As a zombie, you'd be too afraid to ever travel anywhere. You'd be stuck inside your cave forever!

At least I'd be happy inside the cave, not spending every day being terrorized by fish.

VARIATIONS

SEE IF YOU'D CHANGE YOUR DECISION WITH EACH PAIR OF VARIATIONS BELOW.

ZOMBIE AFRAID OF THE DARK	DROWNED AFRAID OF FISH
■ The other zombies feel snubbed by your rejection of the dark and gang up to snuff out your lights.	■ You fight your fear of fish by imagining them all wearing bright pink tutus.
■ You invent a potion of Love to combat your fear but fall in love with the moon instead. Now you travel the Overworld, chasing the night, though it still terrifies you!	■ After you laugh too much at the fish because of their imaginary tutus, they turn against you. Now they gang up and attack you on sight.

77

ALEX AND STEVE ARE RUNNING AROUND IN A PANIC. THE CAVE THEY'VE MADE THEIR LATEST BASE IN IS ABOUT TO COLLAPSE. THEY ONLY HAVE TIME TO PACK UP EITHER THEIR ENCHANTING LIBRARY OR THEIR BREWING ROOM.

WOULD YOU RATHER . . .

be able to enchant anything but not be able to craft potions

OR

craft any potion but never be able to enchant anything?

Quick, help me grab all the potions and glass bottles! It took weeks to find the rare ingredients to craft those.

ALEX

STEVE

No, the enchanting library is more important. It took me forever to collect and craft all those bookshelves!

Who cares about books? I had to face blazes to get the blaze rods for the brewing stand. I would rather never see them again!

Blazes?! I had to mine countless blocks to find the diamond for the enchanting table. And I had to find even more diamonds to be able to mine obsidian, too!

VARIATIONS

SEE IF YOU'D CHANGE YOUR DECISION WITH EACH PAIR OF VARIATIONS BELOW.

ENCHANT ANYTHING	CRAFT ANY POTION
■ You can enchant any item, but your food is enchanted with Unbreaking, taking you twice as long to eat and making your food twice as bland.	■ You can use everything as potion ingredients, but you must taste test any new ingredient you find—even the really gross ones!
■ You can get a level ten enchantment, but it's so powerful that you're magically drawn toward lava.	■ You can now make tasty edible potions, but they all use slimy spider eyes.

79

STEVE AND ALEX HAVE BEEN INVITED TO A COSTUME PARTY, AND THE THEME IS HOSTILE MOBS. STEVE CAN'T DECIDE WHAT TO WEAR.

WOULD YOU RATHER ...

have the horns of a warden

OR

have the tusks of a piglin?

STEVE

I'm going to take the tusks of a piglin. Those tusks will make me look ferocious!

ALEX

Aren't piglin tusks basically extra teeth? I already spend too long brushing my teeth! I'd go for the warden horns. They'll look fierce!

You would need to clean the warden horns, too. Imagine how many cobwebs you'll catch with those on your head!

True, but suddenly having tusks when I'm not used to them would make me drool a lot!

VARIATIONS

SEE IF YOU'D CHANGE YOUR DECISION WITH EACH PAIR OF VARIATIONS BELOW.

WARDEN HORNS	PIGLIN TUSKS
■ Warden horns give you incredible hearing, but you can't fall asleep at night because of the groaning of zombies outside.	■ You can't get used to the new tusks, and it makes drinking anything impossible without spilling it. You now wear a bib.
■ You're now a part of the horned mob gang and can call upon other horned mobs for aid.	■ You form an a cappella group with the piglins. Your tight-knit group travels together everywhere.

81

ALEX AND STEVE ARE READY FOR ANOTHER SURVIVAL CHALLENGE, BUT NEED YOUR HELP DECIDING WHAT TO TRY NEXT!

WOULD YOU RATHER...

have infinite potions but be unable to collect anything else in your inventory

OR

have infinite diamonds but the inability to gain experience?

Not having anything but potions in my inventory would be super difficult. How can you survive without equipment? With infinite diamonds, I'd be able to trade with villagers for anything I needed!

ALEX

STEVE

Easier said than done! You need to find the right villagers first. Plus, you'll never have enough experience to ever enchant anything. Boring!

But what will you do with only potions?

Survive, that's what! I'll use potions of Invisibility to run around undetected, potions of Harming to defeat the mobs, and potions of Regeneration to keep my health up!

VARIATIONS

SEE IF YOU'D CHANGE YOUR DECISION WITH EACH PAIR OF VARIATIONS BELOW.

INFINITE POTIONS	INFINITE DIAMONDS
■ You can only use one potion a day.	■ You can only trade with one villager a day.
■ Every potion you take is random, so you have no idea what you're drinking until it's already taken effect.	■ Treasure hunters and bandits hear of your good fortune. They attack you if you stay in one place for more than a day.

STEVE IS COMPLAINING ABOUT
HIS DAY. HE HAD SPENT ALL OF IT
WORKING ON HIS NEW BUILD, BUT
HIS WORK KEPT ON BEING UNDONE
BY A GRIEFING ENDERMAN. ALEX
WASN'T LISTENING. SHE HAD
HEARD ENOUGH CHATTER THAT
DAY FROM A WANDERING TRADER.

WOULD YOU RATHER...

be followed around
by a griefing
Enderman every
time you build

OR

be accompanied
by a very chatty
wandering
trader every
time you travel?

STEVE

Endermen always get in the way! Every time I think I'm done, I see it remove another block from my design.

Have you been followed by a wandering trader before? They're so relentless. They really want you to look at their trades, whether you're interested or not.

ALEX

I can't tell the Enderman to go away, either. If I look into its eyes, it will start to attack me!

The trader's llamas are even more frustrating. I just wanted to chop some wood, and one of them stepped too close. Now they won't stop spitting at me!

VARIATIONS

SEE IF YOU'D CHANGE YOUR DECISION WITH EACH PAIR OF VARIATIONS BELOW.

GRIEFING ENDERMAN	CHATTY TRADER
■ The Enderman randomly replaces some blocks with infested blocks. This causes an endermite infestation in your new base.	■ The chatty trader gets louder and louder. You can no longer hear any hostile mobs approaching you.
■ The Enderman starts building its own house next to yours with the stolen blocks, and you now have a whole family of Endermen living next to you.	■ The wandering trader is desperate for you to buy its goods. When you don't, it starts throwing snowballs at you and pushing you toward hostile mobs.

85

ALEX AND STEVE HAVE JUST NARROWLY AVOIDED DEFEAT BY CREEPERS. BACK IN THE SAFETY OF THEIR BASE, THEY START TO WONDER . . .

WOULD YOU RATHER . . .

have control of an endless army of tamed cats

OR

have infinite allied creepers at your disposal?

With an army of cats, I'd never have to worry about creepers again.

ALEX

What will you do with an army of cats? They don't attack anything other than chickens, rabbits, and baby turtles. Think of the baby turtles, Alex!

STEVE

Okay, I guess I couldn't have baby turtles around. Worth it for the cats! They scare away both creepers and phantoms. I'd never have to sleep again.

I'd rather have creepers under my control. I could use them for mining. Or if anyone dares mess with my base, I can send them to blow up theirs!

VARIATIONS

SEE IF YOU'D CHANGE YOUR DECISION WITH EACH PAIR OF VARIATIONS BELOW.

ARMY OF CATS	ALLIED CREEPERS
■ Your cat population draws the attention of cat lovers around the Overworld. Witches start coming to your base to steal your fur babies.	■ You can't tell creeper friend from foe. Attack the wrong creeper, and they'll all desert you.
■ You wake up every morning to numerous gifts of rotten flesh left by the cats. You can't leave your base until you've cleaned it all up.	■ The creepers hiss away all night at top volume. Sleeping is almost impossible.

87

ALEX AND STEVE HAVE FINALLY FOUND A RARE AND POWERFUL POTION BOOK THAT WILL ALLOW THEM TO CHANGE THEIR BLOCKY FORMS INTO FORMIDABLE MOBS. THE QUESTION IS, WHAT FORM SHOULD THEY CHOOSE?

WOULD YOU RATHER . . .

be able to morph at will into a super-speedy baby zombie

OR

become a super-strong iron golem?

With the strength of an iron golem, nothing will stand in my way.

ALEX

Nothing except low structures! At three blocks tall, you won't be able to go inside most buildings. As a tiny baby zombie, I can squeeze through narrow gaps easily.

STEVE

Your super-speedy form will have nothing on my super-strong body. I bet that I can mine obsidian in a few hits. I might even break bedrock!

What mount can carry an iron golem? I can ride a chicken and get around even faster!

VARIATIONS

SEE IF YOU'D CHANGE YOUR DECISION WITH EACH PAIR OF VARIATIONS BELOW.

SPEEDY BABY ZOMBIE	STRONG IRON GOLEM
■ You ride a chicken for too long. and it refuses to let you ride it anymore, throwing eggs at you whenever you go near.	■ Your iron form gets rusty when it's wet. You can only move at half speed when it's raining.
■ If you stay a baby zombie for too long, your body will start to zombify for good.	■ If you're an iron golem for too long, your body will begin to crack, and you won't be able to turn back.

89

ALEX AND STEVE ARE EXPLORING A SWAMP BIOME. THEY SEE A WITCH'S HUT AND DECIDE TO INVESTIGATE. INSIDE THEY FIND A BOOK AND QUILL ON THE TABLE WHERE THE WITCH HAS WRITTEN THE MOST BIZARRE QUESTION . . .

WOULD YOU RATHER . . .

have the head of a frog but the body of a witch

OR

the head of a witch on the body of a frog?

STEVE

Wait a second. If I had the head of a frog, would I have to eat small slimes? Gross!

ALEX

But think of all the cool potions you could brew and throw with a witch's body!

I'd still choose the frog body. Think of how high I could jump!

I'd rather have the frog's long, sticky tongue. It could be handy for grabbing things from far away.

VARIATIONS

SEE IF YOU'D CHANGE YOUR DECISION WITH EACH PAIR OF VARIATIONS BELOW.

WITCH BODY, FROG HEAD	FROG BODY, WITCH HEAD
■ Whenever you see a small slime, you can't think of anything else until you have devoured it.	■ You're called to battle alongside illagers every time there's a village raid in your biome.
■ You take a special potion of Strength, which allows you to swing from tree to tree using your tongue.	■ You invent a new potion of Camouflage, which enables you to change the color of your body at will like a chameleon.

91

STEVE AND ALEX ARE ARGUING ABOUT WHO IS THE BETTER ENDER DRAGON SLAYER.

BOTH MAKE SOME BOLD CLAIMS ABOUT THEIR ABILITIES.

WOULD YOU RATHER . . .

fight an Ender Dragon with just a Strength potion and no weapons

OR

fight with an Infinity-enchanted bow while inflicted with Nausea?

92

STEVE

As soon as the Ender Dragon flies near me, I'll smack it on the nose so hard with my fists, it will be seeing two of me.

Hitting the Ender Dragon up close isn't easy! With my enchanted bow, I can keep shooting as many arrows as I like until it's defeated.

ALEX

You won't hit many targets while nauseated; it makes your vision wobbly!

I'll have the Infinity enchantment, and I'll just keep shooting! Getting near an Ender Dragon, even with a potion of Strength, could be fatal!

VARIATIONS

SEE IF YOU'D CHANGE YOUR DECISION WITH EACH PAIR OF VARIATIONS BELOW.

STRENGTH POTION	INFINITY-ENCHANTED BOW
▪ Every time you punch the Ender Dragon, it retaliates with a flick of its tail sending you flying across the arena.	▪ For every arrow you shoot that misses the Ender Dragon, your nausea continues for an extra ten ticks.
▪ Giving up on your fists, you begin breakdancing. Now the fight is an epic dance battle, and the Ender Dragon has some killer moves!	▪ Once your nausea subsides, you can see clearly: You shouldn't be fighting with violence. You should be singing! The Ender Dragon has a surprising set of lungs.

STEVE AND ALEX YAWN AS THEY
GET READY TO SLEEP. THE PAIR
HAVE JUST COMPLETED TWO
BACK-TO-BACK ADVENTURES AND
NEITHER WENT QUITE AS PLANNED.
IN HINDSIGHT, THEY SHOULD HAVE
DONE JUST ONE.

WOULD YOU RATHER...

be debuffed with
Mining Fatigue
while searching an
ocean monument

OR

be hit by
Levitation
while searching
an End city?

That Mining Fatigue really slowed me down!
I wanted to break into the monument from
the top, but I couldn't mine the prismarine
with the negative status effect.

ALEX

STEVE

Levitating up into the void
of the End is terrifying.
The only place to go is back
down! At least underwater,
you want to move upward.

You still had the ability to fight when you were
on the ground—that Mining Fatigue slowed
down my attacks and left me vulnerable!

At least you could use a bucket of milk to remove your
status effect. It would have worked for me, too. But by
the time I was up in the air, it was a little too late!

VARIATIONS

SEE IF YOU'D CHANGE YOUR DECISION WITH EACH
PAIR OF VARIATIONS BELOW.

MINING FATIGUE IN AN OCEAN MONUMENT	LEVITATION IN AN END CITY
■ You leave your pet cow in the boat, but it's a scaredy-cow. If you leave it alone for more than 30 ticks, it will capsize the boat.	■ You brought a cow with you to the End, but the Ender Dragon soon gobbled it up. You did manage to milk it first though!
■ Dolphins come along to chase away the guardians, but this only attracts the attention of elder guardians.	■ Endermen decide to heroically pluck you from the sky. They teleport you eight blocks away—potentially over the void!

95

ALEX AND STEVE GET BACK FROM THE END DIMENSION. HAVING NOW VISITED BOTH THE END AND THE NETHER, THEY WONDER WHICH ONE THEY'D RISK GETTING TRAPPED IN.

WOULD YOU RATHER ...

be stuck in the End fighting the Ender Dragon over and over

OR

be trapped in the Nether being constantly hunted by a gang of piglin brutes?

STEVE

The Ender Dragon is one of the fiercest mobs in the game—it can fly, not to mention the fact that it breathes fire!

But surely it's easier to hide from one mob than it is from several mobs.

ALEX

But if you're stuck facing that same mob over and over, isn't that worse? There is more space to run in the Nether. The Ender Dragon's island is big, but it's also inhabited by Endermen.

As long as I keep my pumpkin head on, they'll leave me alone. In the Nether, you will run into more mobs and dangers if you try to hide—not to mention lava, if you don't look where you're going!

VARIATIONS

SEE IF YOU'D CHANGE YOUR DECISION WITH EACH PAIR OF VARIATIONS BELOW.

ENDER DRAGON	PIGLIN BRUTES
■ You have a pumpkin head, so the Endermen will leave you alone, but this only makes the Ender Dragon hungry for pumpkin-and-player pie!	■ You befriend a strider that helps you get around the Nether, but the piglin brutes are able to track you whenever you're riding it.
■ Every time you defeat the Ender Dragon, an End gateway portal opens, giving you just enough time to access some loot.	■ You collect enough blaze rods to build a brewing stand and craft potions that make the piglin brutes easier to defeat.

97

CRASH! A CLUMSY ENDERMAN HAS KNOCKED OVER STEVE'S CHEST OF PRIZED POSSESSIONS, WHICH HE CARELESSLY LEFT ON THE EDGE OF A BADLANDS MESA. LEAPING FORWARD, HE IS ONLY FAST ENOUGH TO SAVE ONE ITEM.

WOULD YOU RATHER...

save a pair of boots that allow you to fly

OR

save a helmet that makes you invisible?

VARIATIONS

SEE IF YOU'D CHANGE YOUR DECISION WITH EACH PAIR OF VARIATIONS BELOW.

BOOTS FOR FLYING

- The boots are mega uncomfortable, so you can't walk on land in them.
- The boots only let you fly for 30 seconds before making you fall from whatever height you're at.

HELMET FOR INVISIBILITY

- The helmet is too small and impairs your eyesight when you wear it.
- The helmet only makes you invisible for 30 seconds, and then you glow like a beacon that attracts all nearby hostile mobs.

STEVE: Those boots would save me from being chased by many mobs on land. Flying would allow me to explore more than I ever could on foot.

ALEX: The helmet would keep me safe from mobs almost everywhere. But the helmet would give me the freedom to search temples and pyramids peacefully.

ALEX AND STEVE ARE PLANNING A NEIGHBORHOOD BLOCK PARTY. THEY'VE INCLUDED A FEW PARTY GAMES FOR THEIR GUESTS, BUT THEY'RE NOT QUITE GOING TO PLAN.

WOULD YOU RATHER...

play hide-and-seek with a charged creeper

OR

play sardines with ten baby zombies?

STEVE

ALEX

Throwing a party seemed like such a good idea. But did you have to invite *those* neighbors?

They weren't exactly invited. . . .

Well, playing hide-and-seek with a charged creeper is sure to end the party with a bang.

But then sardines requires I sit with nine wriggly baby zombies until the tenth manages to find us. I'm not sure I'd survive that!

VARIATIONS

SEE IF YOU'D CHANGE YOUR DECISION WITH EACH PAIR OF VARIATIONS BELOW.

HIDE-AND-SEEK	SARDINES
▪ The charged creeper gives you a three-second head start once it's found you before it inevitably explodes.	▪ The baby zombies agree to be passive until the last one finds you. Then all bets are off, and you must fight them!
▪ The charged creeper brings its creeper friends to drop some killer beats and provide an epic soundtrack for your game.	▪ The baby zombies have bred a giant chicken for you to ride while playing the game with them.

101

STEVE GASPS. HE HAS JUST WOKEN UP FROM A DREAM ABOUT AN EPIC BATTLE. AN EVIL EVOKER WAS CHANTING INCANTATIONS, THEN SOMETHING UNBELIEVABLE STARTED HAPPENING TO THE MOBS!

WOULD YOU RATHER . . .

be a giant zombie vs. ten creepers

OR

be a giant creeper vs. ten baby zombies ?

The giant zombie's greatest strength is also its greatest weakness—its size. It's so big, the creepers will have no trouble hitting it.

ALEX

STEVE

But a creeper's greatest strength is also the thing that defeats it: its only attack is exploding.

But at that size, all it would need to do is tread on all those baby zombies!

It would have to catch them first! Never underestimate the speed of a baby zombie.

VARIATIONS

SEE IF YOU'D CHANGE YOUR DECISION WITH EACH PAIR OF VARIATIONS BELOW.

GIANT ZOMBIE	GIANT CREEPER
■ The giant zombie starts breaking out some stomping dance moves, crushing its opponents on the dance floor.	■ The giant creeper lights up like a disco ball dazzling the baby zombies until they are almost blind.
■ A thunderstorm strikes, and the remaining creepers become charged. One blow is all it will take to defeat you.	■ The baby zombies summon their mutant creeper-eating chickens and ride them boldly into battle!

103

STEVE HAS BEEN EVERYWHERE AND SEEN EVERYTHING IN MINECRAFT, AND IS CONVINCED THERE ARE NO NEW CHALLENGES LEFT. NEVER ONE TO ACCEPT DEFEAT, ALEX COMES UP WITH TWO NEW ONES FOR HIM TO CHOOSE FROM.

WOULD YOU RATHER . . .

explore the End with unlimited food

OR

explore with unlimited Ender pearls in your inventory?

Too easy. With unlimited food I can keep searching until I find the End city, taking it one block at a time.

The End is full of dangers, though. If you get struck by a shulker, food won't stop you from floating off.

STEVE

ALEX

But there's next to no food in the End. Chorus fruit is hardly an option when it teleports you at random!

At least your Ender pearls will teleport you back!

If I'm not already lost to the abyss!

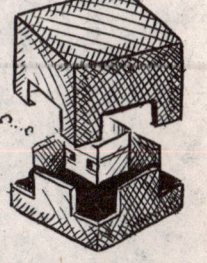

VARIATIONS

SEE IF YOU'D CHANGE YOUR DECISION WITH EACH PAIR OF VARIATIONS BELOW.

UNLIMITED FOOD	UNLIMITED ENDER PEARLS
■ Shulker bullets can travel twice as fast while you eat.	■ Every thrown Ender pearl spawns an endermite.
■ Eating in the End offends the Endermen that come to attack you every time you eat.	■ You can only move by using an Ender pearl. Be sure to throw them accurately!

105

STEVE AND ALEX HAVE BOTH WOUND UP IN DESPERATE SITUATIONS. STEVE NEEDS TO RUN THROUGH A THUNDERSTORM TO SAVE HIS BASE, WHILE ALEX NEEDS GOLD IN THE PIGLIN-INFESTED NETHER.

WOULD YOU RATHER . . .

stand in a thunderstorm holding a lightning rod

OR

mine gold in front of a piglin?

We need another gold ingot, but the closest place to find one is in the Nether! We haven't got time to risk bartering so we'll just have to mine in front of them.

ALEX

STEVE

We haven't got time to find redstone ore, either. We will need to use the lightning storm to power the mechanism.

A lightning rod would work, but it will electrify whoever is holding it and also deal a lot of damage.

Piglins are very protective of gold. They won't be happy to see you mining it in front of them!

VARIATIONS

SEE IF YOU'D CHANGE YOUR DECISION WITH EACH PAIR OF VARIATIONS BELOW.

HOLD A LIGHTNING ROD	MINE GOLD
■ The thunderstorm flashes, striking mobs around you. You now have zombified piglins and witches surrounding you.	■ You capture the attention of piglin brutes that are furious you'd be so brazen as to mine for gold on their land.
■ You have a potion of Healing ready to fix some of the damage from the lightning strike.	■ You have a potion of Swiftness to hightail it out of the Nether once you have your gold ingot.

107

ALEX AND STEVE HAVE STUMBLED
UPON A STRUCTURE PROTECTED
BY MANY TRAPS. AFTER HOURS OF
TRYING, THEY BREAK IN TO FIND AN
IMPRISONED WITCH THAT OFFERS A
REWARD FOR FREEING THEM.

WOULD YOU RATHER . . .

be able to breathe fire but be trapped in the ground until someone triggers a skulk sensor

OR

have the warden's sonic boom but explode every time you see an Enderman?

ALEX

Being trapped in the ground sounds terribly boring! Who knows how long it would take for someone to trigger a sculk sensor and release me. I'd take the sonic boom! I'd be invincible!

STEVE

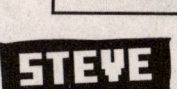

But exploding every time you see an Enderman will make your travels very difficult. They're in every dimension and can appear at any moment. At least with dragon fire, you'd be free once you escape.

VARIATIONS

SEE IF YOU'D CHANGE YOUR DECISION WITH EACH PAIR OF VARIATIONS BELOW.

BREATHE FIRE	HAVE SONIC BOOM
■ Once you're released, a renowned dragon slayer hears of your reputation. It stands outside your base every morning, challenging you to a duel.	■ An Enderman teleports to your side once a day. It dances around, goading you to sneak a peek at it. You must defeat it without looking at it.
■ Every day, you must win a challenge or be trapped underground again. Today you must beat a villager at making a cake, using only your fire to bake it.	■ A haggle of Endermen keep on griefing your base each day. You can either explode and be done with them or let them dismantle your home forever.

109

CREATE YOUR OWN WOULD YOU RATHER

1. CHOOSE YOUR THEME

Every great Would You Rather has a theme. What's your favorite aspect of Minecraft? It could be anything from a particular mob to an activity or even a biome's characteristics.

2. BRAINSTORM IDEAS

Write down anything funny or interesting that comes to mind when you think of your theme, then write down their opposites.

3. WRITE THE WOULD YOU RATHER

Now that you have some ideas and their opposites, it's time to put them together to form your question. The best Would You Rathers are balanced, so that there's no clear choice and can include opposing pros and cons.

4. CREATE VARIATIONS

How can you add to the options to make your debate even harder or funnier? Create variations for both sides of your debate—some that make the situation better or funnier, and some that make it harder.

EXAMPLE

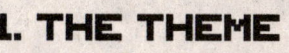

1. THE THEME

Villagers

2. BRAINSTORM IDEAS

Villagers are over-friendly and offer great trade prices vs. villagers won't talk or trade with you.

Villagers letting their pigs into your vegetable patch vs. villagers tending to your vegetable patch.

3. WRITE THE WOULD YOU RATHER

live in a village where the villagers offer you great prices, but their pigs have a nasty habit of eating all your vegetables

OR

settle where none of the villagers will trade with you, but the farmers tend to your vegetable patches for you?

4. CREATE VARIATIONS

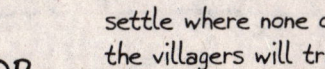

■ The villagers wake you up every morning with a loud song of friendship that is both super annoying and mega catchy.

■ If you look at a villager for more than ten seconds, it will set the village iron golem on you!

Why not debate your favorite scenarios with your friends or family? You might be surprised by their responses!

Q

A

MY HUMOR

Write your own Minecraft jokes, puns, and riddles!

Q _____
_____
_____
_____

A _____
_____
_____
_____

Q

A

MY HUMOR

Write your own Minecraft jokes, puns, and riddles!

Q. _____

_____

_____

_____

A. _____

_____

_____

_____

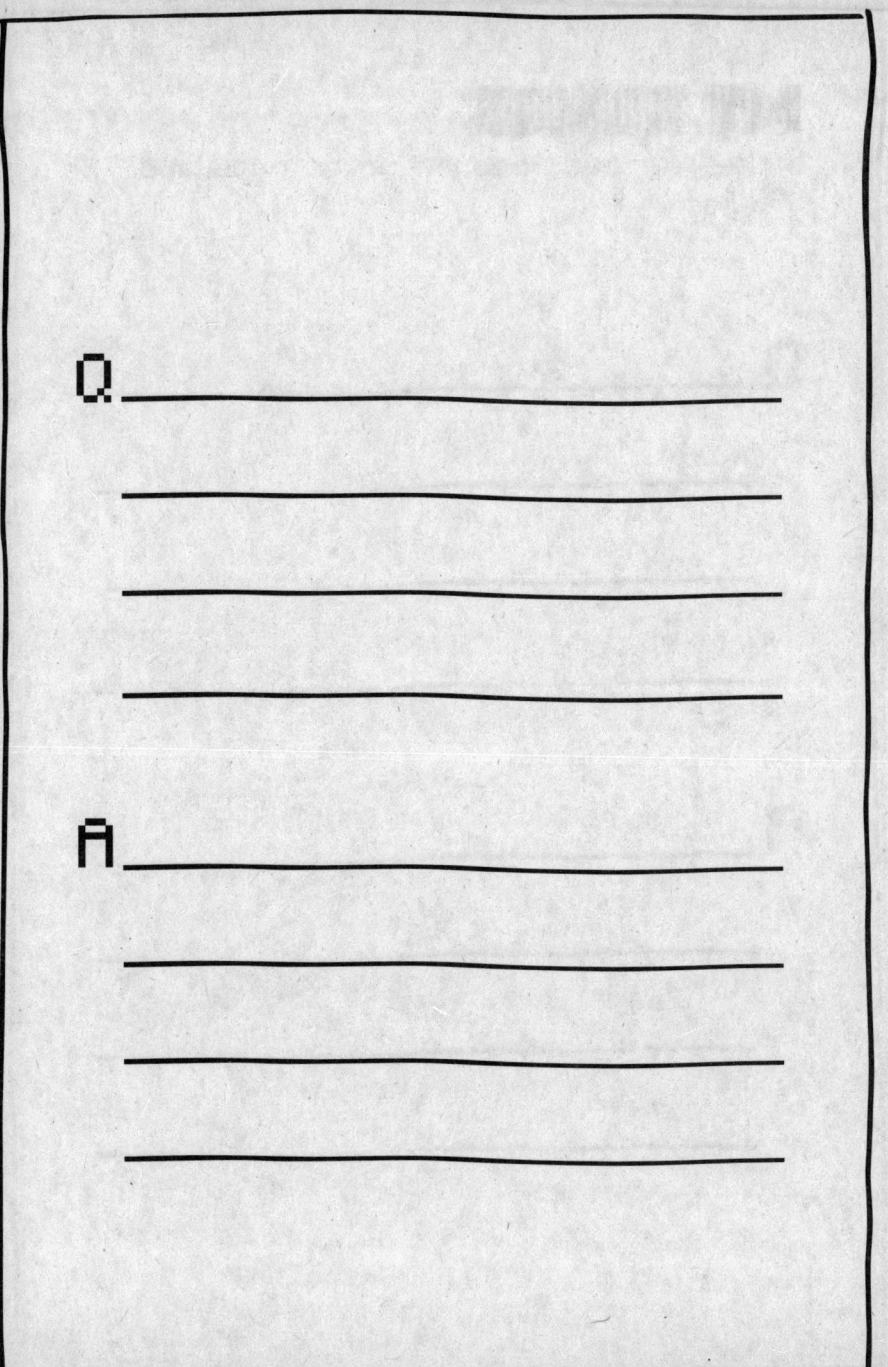

MY HUMOR

Write your own Minecraft jokes, puns, and riddles!

Q _____

_____

_____

_____

A _____

_____

_____

_____

MY NUMBER

Q

A

MY HUMOR

Write your own Minecraft jokes, puns, and riddles!

Q _____

_____

_____

_____

_____

A _____

_____

_____

_____

_____

Q What's so special about dragon eggs?

A They're eggs-cellent, of course!

Q Which ball shouldn't you play with?

A A dragon's fireball.

Q What do you say to the ender dragon on its birthday?

A Flappy birthday!

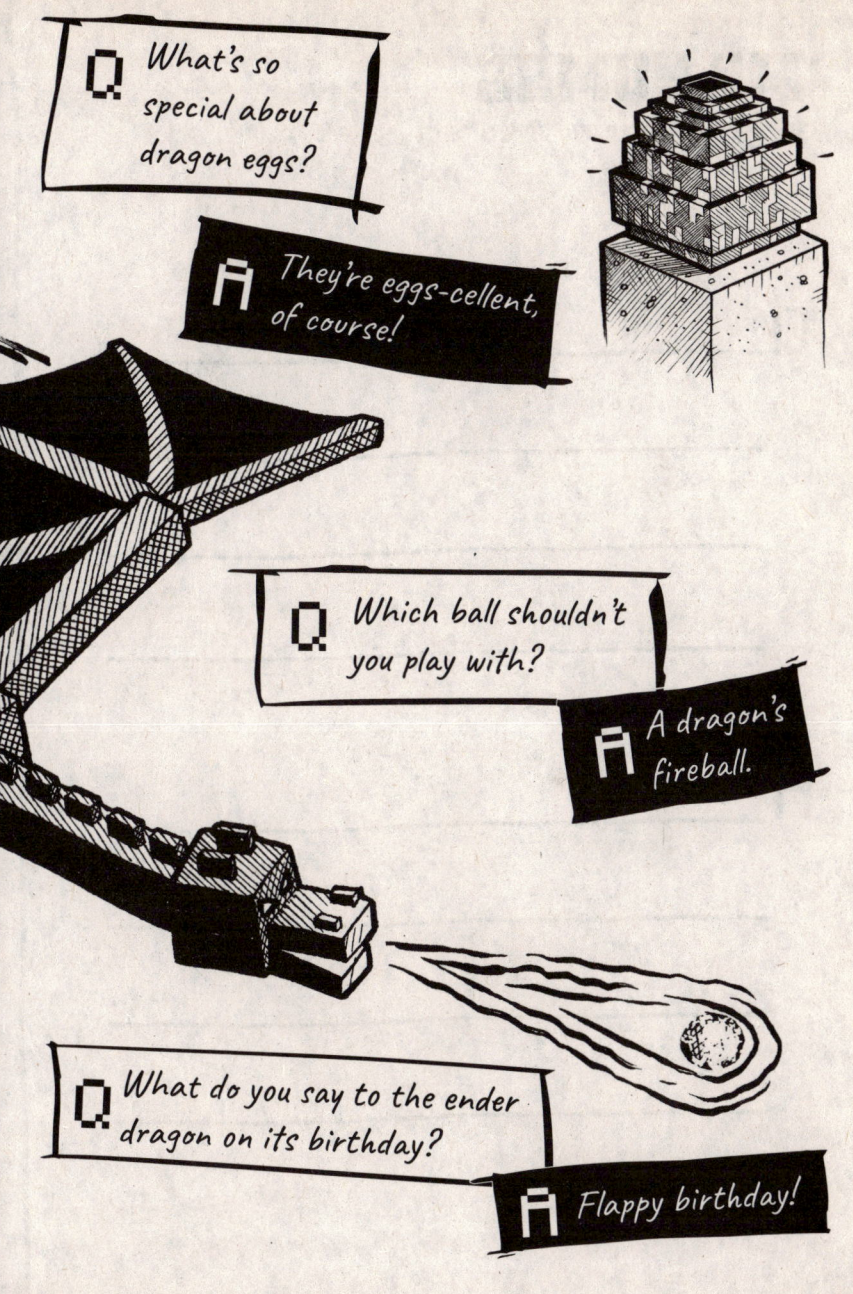

REPTILE ROARS

Read these jokes to make the ender dragon seem less scary!

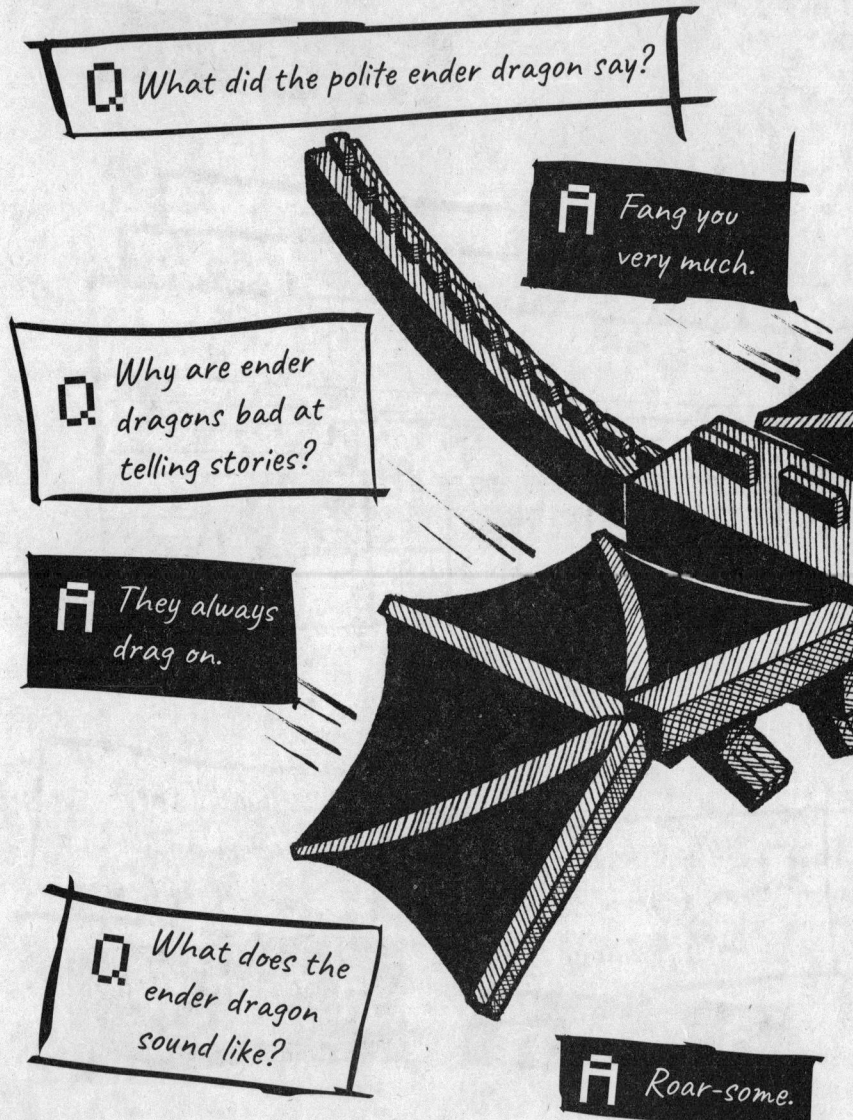

Q What did the polite ender dragon say?

A Fang you very much.

Q Why are ender dragons bad at telling stories?

A They always drag on.

Q What does the ender dragon sound like?

A Roar-some.

Q: What do you call it when Steve dresses up as an enderman?

A: A pretenderman.

Q: What do you call an enderman with feelings?

A: A tenderman.

Q: Why did the enderman live in a one-story house?

A: Because it didn't like stares.

ALMOST AT THE END...ERMAN

These jokes will teleport you to the funny dimension.

Q What do you call a group of endermen?

A An enderclan.

Q What do you get if you cross an enderman and a village priest?

A An end-amen.

Q What do you call an enderman that has lost weight?

A A slenderman.

Q Why didn't the enderman cross the road?

A Because it teleported across instead.

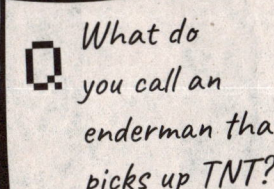

Q What do you call an enderman that picks up TNT?

A Extremely dangerous.

ENDERMANIA!
These jokes are a scream!

Q Why don't endermen like jokes about water?

A They only like dry humor.

Q Where do endermen sleep?

A Anywhere they like.

Q Why are endermen so tall?

A Because their feet smell.

Q When does bread rise?

A When you yeast expect it.

Q What did the angry cake say to Alex and Steve?

A You wanna piece of me?

Q Did you hear about the pumpkin pie that ran away?

A It desserted.

Q Did you hear about the villager that was stealing food?

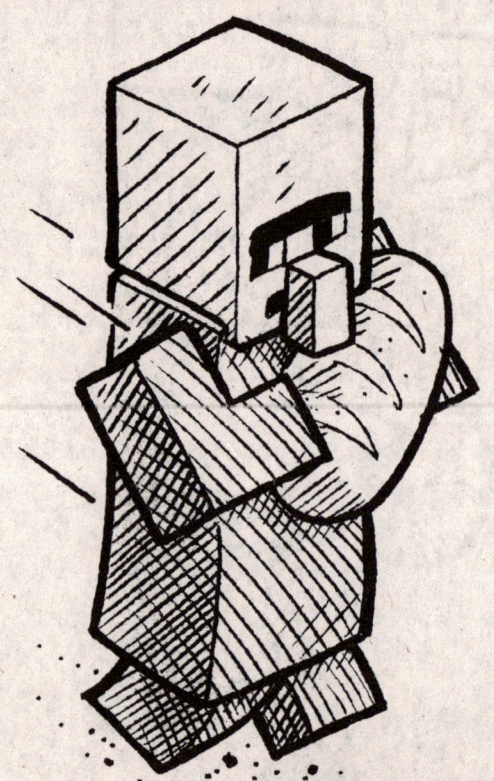

A It was caught bread-handed.

HALF-BAKED HUMOR

We hope these hot cross *puns* get a rise out of you.

Q: What did Alex say to the tasty bread?

A: I loaf you.

Q What do you call a messy cat?

A A shabby tabby.

Q Why is it hard for ocelots to hide?

A Because they're always spotted.

Q What do you call a pile of kittens?

A A meow-ntain.

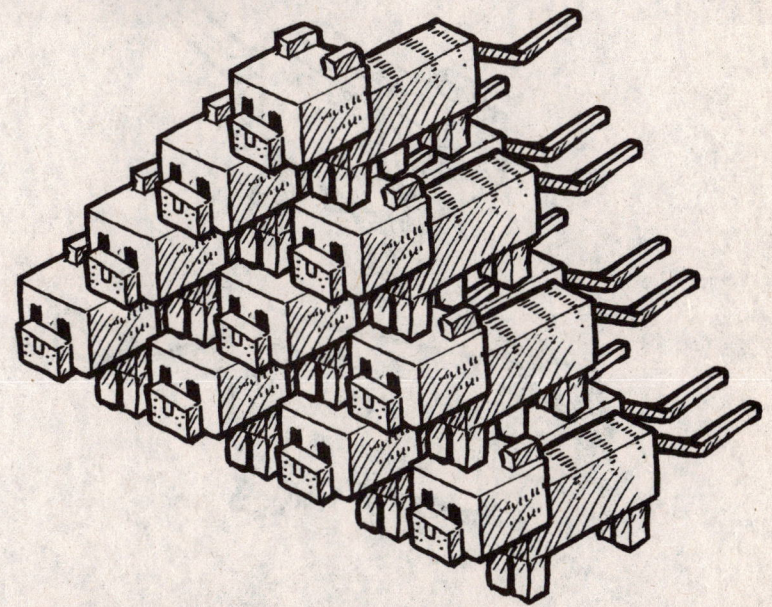

Q How do you know when a cat is hurt?

A It says, "Me-OW."

PET PUNS

Wolf down these purr-fect puns.

Q What did the skeleton say to the wolf?

A Bone appétit.

Q What do you get if you cross a wolf with a sheep?

A A wolf in sheep's clothing.

Q Did you hear about the minecart that lost control?

A It really went off the rails.

Q How do you find a missing minecart?

A Just follow the tracks.

Q Why was the minecart late?

A It got sidetracked.

Steve: How many minecarts came off the rails?

Alex: I don't know, it's hard to keep track.

MINE, ALL MINE!
Get back on track with this minecart full of cheer.

Q Did you hear about the player who used a potion of Invisibility while taking a ride in a minecart?

A She was trying to cover her tracks.

Q Why was the minecart so late?

A It really got off track.

THE END OF THE END
Stop dragon your heels and read on!

Q Why are shulkers bad at telling jokes?

A Because they always start at the End.

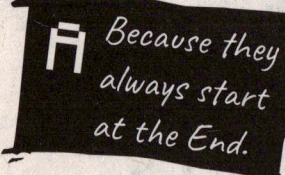

Q Why do shulkers hide in their shells?

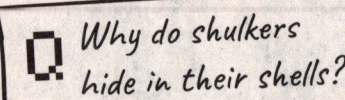

A Because they're shulking.

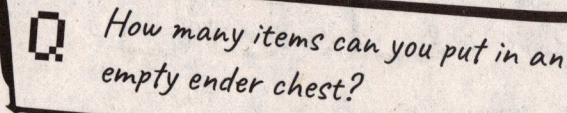

Q How many items can you put in an empty ender chest?

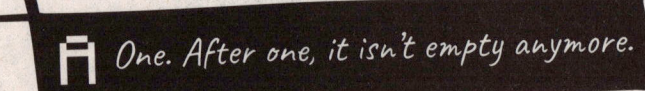

A One. After one, it isn't empty anymore.

Q What do you call an endermite that can't make up its mind?

A An ender-might.

Q Why do cats like End cities?

A Because they're made from purrpurr blocks.

IN THE END

To get to these jokes, you'll need to find a chortle room.

Q What's the last block you should place when you finish a build?

A The End stone.

Q Why did Steve think the shulker was shy?

A Because it wouldn't come out of its shell.

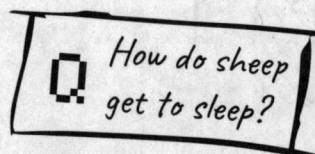
Q How do sheep get to sleep?

A They count themselves.

Q: What play do pigs love?

A: Hamlet.

Q: What do you call a pig with three eyes?

A: A piiig.

FARMYARD FUNNIES

Have a giggle at these farmyard funnies.

Q Why do cows prefer the other side?

A Because the grass is always greener.

Q Did you hear about the giant cow in the tiny house?

A There wasn't mooshroom.

Q Why did the witch write a book?

A Because it was good at spelling.

Q Why is it easy to confuse one witch with another?

A Because it's hard to tell which witch is which.

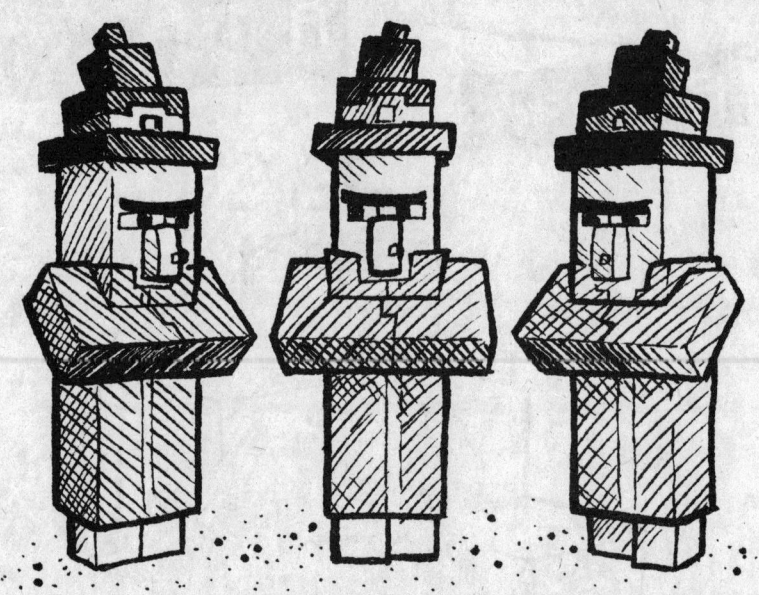

Q What do you call a witch in a hole?

A A ditch.

WITTY WITCHES
These jokes will really make you cackle!

Q What do you call a witch covered in sand?

A A sand-witch.

Q Why did the witches stop being friends?

A They were driving each other batty.

Q What do you call a witch that won't stop scratching?

A An itch.

Q How do you deal with a group of hostile llamas?

A You just have to get used to spit.

Q Why are polar bears bad at conversation?

A They're afraid to break the ice.

Q What do polar bears eat for lunch?

A Icebergers.

FLUFFY FUNNIES

They might both have fluffy white coats, but mix up the polar bear and the llama at your peril!

Steve: Did you see the animal film last night?

Alex: No, what did I miss?

Steve: Just some llama drama.

Q What did the llama say when it was told to leave the village?

A Alpaca my bags.

Q What do you call a polar bear in the desert?

A Lost.

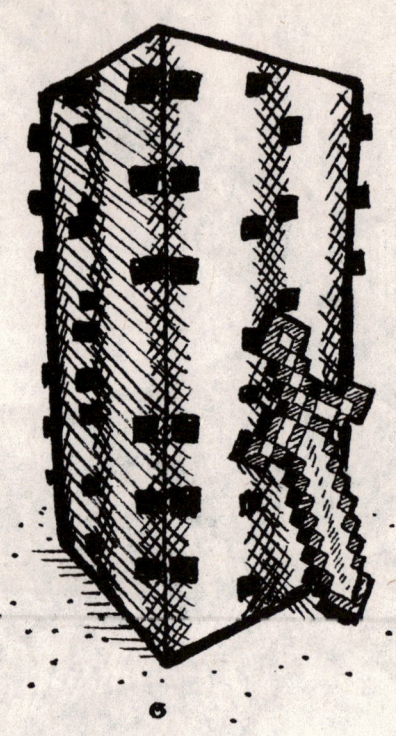

Q: What's a cactus's favorite enchantment?

A: Sharpness.

Q Which enchantment hurts flying mobs?

A Ender-smite.

WIT AND WIZARDRY

Combine an enchantment with this book to magic up some laughs.

Q: Which flower is like an enchantment?

A: A rosebush, because it has thorns.

Q: Which enchantment makes fish faster?

A: Ef-fish-ciency.

Q What has four legs and goes BOOM?

A Two players fighting over a block of TNT.

Q Why are explosions in the rain depressing?

A It's all boom and gloom.

Q What do you get if you cross a clock with TNT?

A A ticking time bomb.

TNT TITTERS

3, 2, 1 . . . get ready to blow your top with giggles.

Q Did you hear about the argument between the building and the TNT?

A It was blown out of proportion.

Q What did Alex say when she lost her TNT?

A Oh, blast.

Q: What do you get when you cross a creeper and a spider?

A: A creepy crawly.

Q Did you hear about the undercover arachnid?

A It was a spy-der.

Q Why did the spider buy a laptop?

A Because it wanted to build a website.

Q Why are spiders good swimmers?

A Because they have webbed feet.

ARACHNID ANTICS

These jokes could make you scream with laughter or terror!

Q How did Steve know the spider was angry?

A It was crawling up the wall.

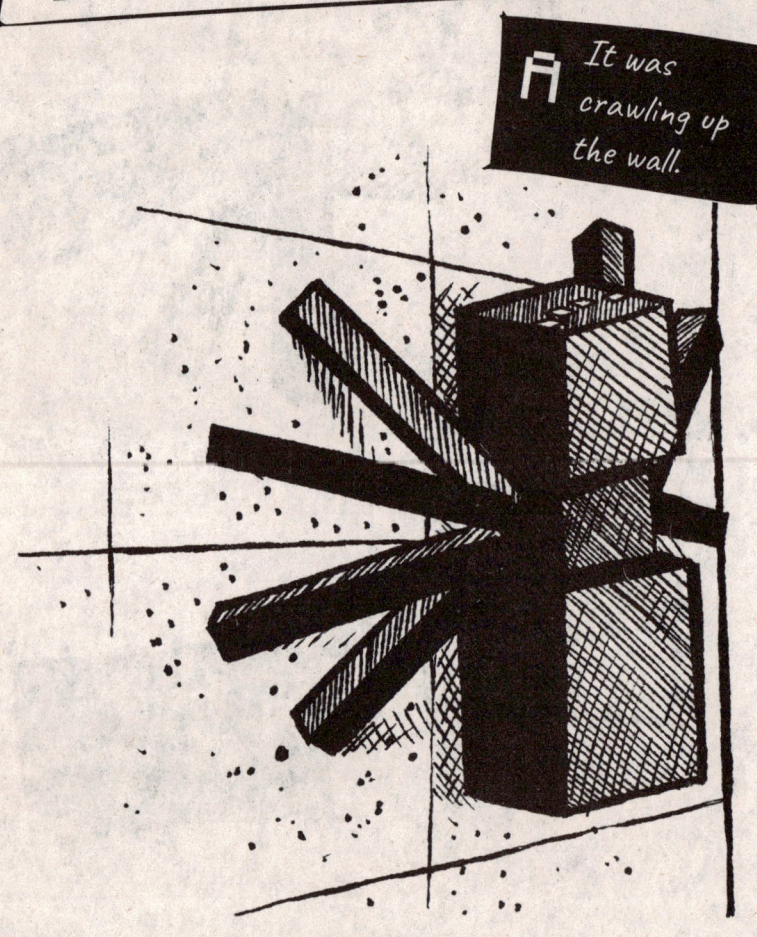

Q What do you get if you cross a cave spider with a cookie?

A I'm not sure, but I wouldn't try eating it.

Q What do you get if you cross a spider and a chicken?

A Webbed feet.

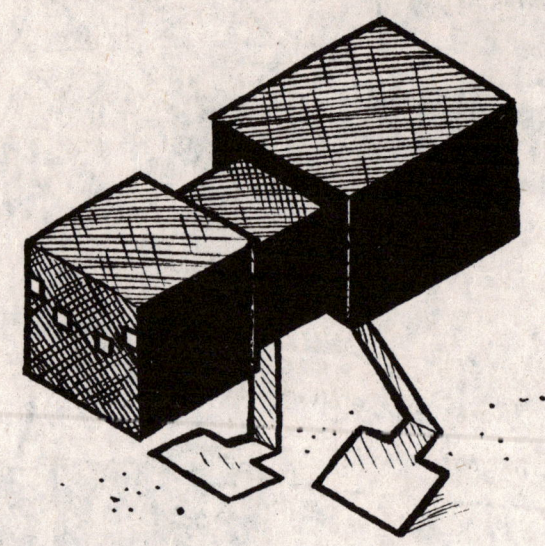

Q Why are spiders such a problem underground?

A Because they scare people out of their mines.

CREEPY CRAWLIES
Hopefully these jokes won't make your skin crawl.

Q What are spiderwebs good for?

A Spiders.

Q What's worse than finding a spider in your base?

A Losing a spider in your base.

Q What music does Steve listen to when he's building?

A Block and roll.

I'd tell you the joke about the roof, but it'd probably go over your head.

Q Did you hear about the builder who built a village on a cliff?

A He liked living on the edge.

CHOCK-A-BLOCK

Building rule number one: don't get stuck between a block and a hard place.

Q Did you hear the great building joke?

A Oh wait, it's not finished yet.

Q How does Steve party when he's finished building?

A He raises the roof.

Q How did the chicken get out of the egg?

A It hatched a plan.

Q What do you get when you cross a creeper with a chicken?

A Eggs-plosions.

JUST WING IT
A little bird told us you like eggs-cellent jokes.

Q What do you get when you cross a parrot with a zombie?

A A bird that talks your head off.

Q What do you get when you cross a spider with a parrot?

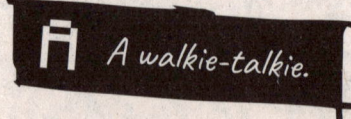

A A walkie-talkie.

Q Did you hear about the player who threw all his potions?

A He really caused a splash.

Q: Why is brewing an enlightening experience?

A: Because of all the glowstone dust.

When Alex saw Steve struggling to make a potion, she knew there was trouble brewing.

Q Where do all the fish sleep?

A On the seabed.

SLEEP ON THESE
These jokes are simply dreamy!

Q Why can't you trust someone sleeping in a bed?

A Because they're lying.

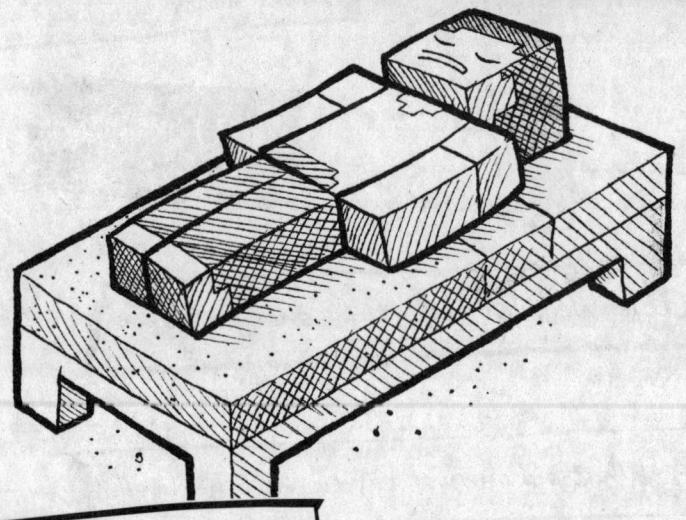

Q Did you hear about the miner who had trouble nodding off?

A He had to rock himself to sleep.

Q Did you hear about the naughty miner who didn't want to sleep?

A He was resisting a rest.

Steve: My recipe book fell on my head.

Alex: That must have hurt.

Steve: Well, I've only got my shelf to blame.

Q What did one wall say to the other wall?

A Meet you at the corner.

Q Did you hear Steve had too many books?

A He never did have any shelf control.

CRAFTY CHUCKLES
Let your laughter build and build.

Q Did you hear about the painter who played Minecraft?

A She was good at arts and crafts.

Q What do you call it when a witch makes something?

A Witchcraft.

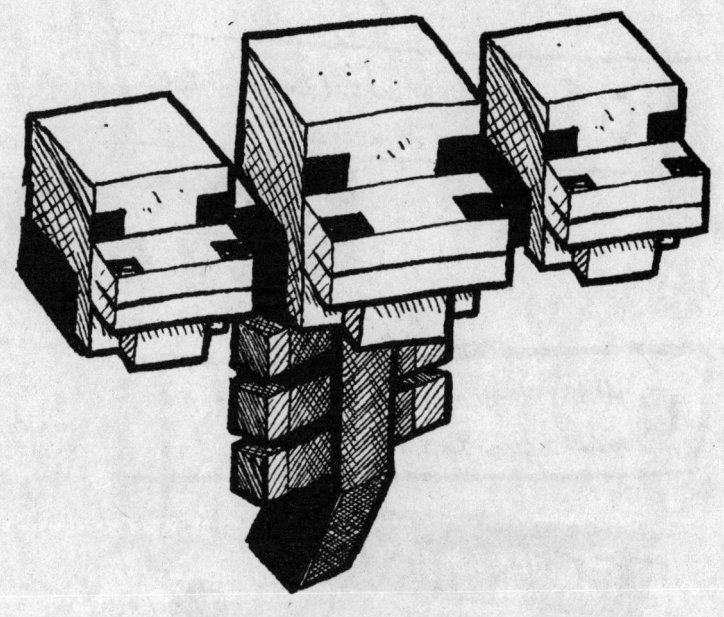

Q *What do you get when you cross a wither with a chicken?*

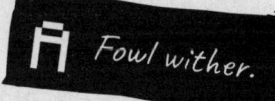

A *Fowl wither.*

Q Why is the wither still single?

A Because it's immune to lava.

Q What do you call the wither in winter?

A A bunch of numbskulls.

LOOKS LIKE BAD WITHER

Here are some more jokes, wither or not you want them!

Q Why is the wither always itchy?

A It has soul sand all over its body.

Q Why are the wither's plans so good?

A Because it can put its three heads together.

Q Have you heard about the enthusiastic sword?

A It always takes a stab at everything.

Q Have you heard about the broken sword?

A It's pointless.

Q. Why are drowned mobs great at throwing tridents?

A. Because they always aim high.

WITTY WEAPONS
Let's hope you get the point with these puns.

Q What did the axe say when it was in a hurry?

A Chop-chop!

Q What did Alex say when Steve held the sword upside down?

A That's not the point.

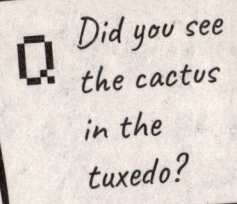

Q: Did you see the cactus in the tuxedo?

A: It was looking sharp.

Q: Which flower grows right under your nose?

A: Tulips.

Q: What do trees put on before swimming?

A: Their trunks.

PLANT PUNS AND FLOWER FUNNIES

These jokes are *blooming* hilarious.

Q What did the flower say when it had a little accident?

A I wet my plants!

Q Did you hear about the panda that lost its bamboo?

A It was bamboo-zled.

Q What do you call a golem that's not there?

A Snow golem.

Q Did you hear about the iron golem that fell in water?

A It got that sinking feeling.

Q What did the iron golem give to the villager's grandfather?

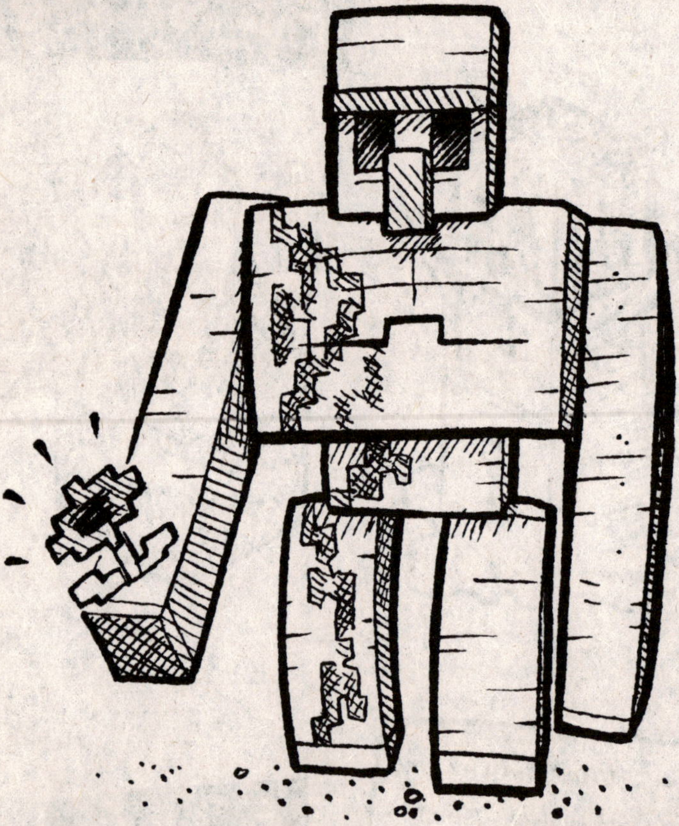

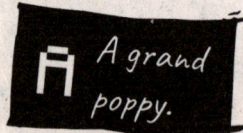

A A grand poppy.

GOLEM GAGS
Make *snow* mistake, these jokes are ironclad.

Q Why can't snow golems play football?

A Snowballs allowed.

Q What did the fire say when it met the snow golem?

A Pleased to melt you.

Q Why was the zombified piglin tired?

A Because it was dead on its feet.

Q Did you hear about the snow golem that spawned in the Nether?

A It had a meltdown.

NETHER AGAIN
Spending time in the Nether is a real scream!

Q Why can't you get a good night's sleep in the Nether?

A Because the beds explode.

Steve: I tried bringing water into the Nether.

Alex: Big mist-take.

Q What do you call it when you get sand on your shoe in the Nether?

A Sole sand.

Q How did Steve feel when he saw that his Nether portal had been destroyed?

A A-ghast.

Q What did Alex say when she returned to the Nether?

A Never say Nether.

INTO THE NETHER
Get ready for some fiery fun!

Q Did you hear about the skeleton that found romance in the Nether?

A It fell head over heels in lava.

Steve: I'm struggling to think of a lava joke.

Alex: You should just let it flow.

Q What did Alex say after she escaped the Nether?

A Nether again.

Q Why do creepers love going to parties?

A Because they always have a blast.

Q Why was the creeper excited when it got hit by lightning?

A It was all charged up.

BOOM BOOM!
Get ready to explode with laughter!

Q: Why are creepers prone to jealousy?

A: Because they're green with envy.

Q: What happened when Alex noticed the creeper was following her?

A: It blew its opportunity.

Q: What do creepers play their music on?

A: A BOOMbox.

Q Why aren't creepers good in arguments?

A They have a short fuse.

Q Why did the creeper cross the road?

A To get to the other sssssside.

Q Did you hear about the creeper's birthday party?

A It really went off with a BANG!

EXPLOSIVE LAUGHS
These jokes will really creep up on you!

Q What is a creeper's favorite subject at school?

A Hisssssstory!

Q What do Australian creepers use to hunt?

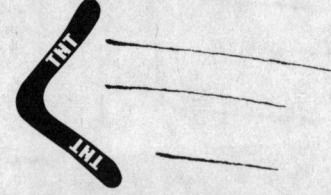

A BOOMerangs.

MINE MANIA

You'll need to dig deep for these belly laughs.

Q: Why couldn't Steve get to the emerald ore?

A: Something was blocking his way.

Q: Where do tired miners sleep?

A: On bedrock.

Q Why won't crops grow in the Nether?

A Because they wither away.

Q How do you fix a pumpkin?

A With a pumpkin patch.

Q Did you hear about the sickly potato?

A It wasn't peeling very well.

Q What do you call it when a pig rolls over a potato?

A Mashed pork-tato.

CROP TO IT!

Plant a smile on your face and let these jokes grow on you.

Q Did you hear about the chicken that ate all the seeds?

A It still felt peck-ish.

Q Why did the chicken stay at home?

A Because it felt fowl.

Q What reminder did Steve write when he needed infinite water?

A Get well soon.

WATER LOTTA LAUGHS

Cry tears of laughter as you read these witty, watery wisecracks.

Q What should you collect icy water in?

A A cold-ron.

Q Why did the fish blush?

A Because it saw the ocean's bottom.

Q Where do the drowned like to swim?

A The Dead Sea.

Q Why are iron ingot-makers always accused of being gassy?

A Because whoever smelt it dealt it.

Q What do gold ore and farts have in common?

A They both smelt.

Q Why is redstone messy?

A Because of all the dust.

Q When were redstone jokes the funniest?

A During the Stone Age.

ORE-FULLY FUNNY
Roar along with these ore-fully good jokes.

Q What did the ore block say to the miner?

A Pick me!

Q How do emeralds exercise?

A Gem-nastics.

Q Why did the Nether quartz ore quit?

A Everyone took it for granite.

Q How did Alex get extra ore?

A With good fortune.

ORE-SOME JOKES
Have a giggle at these gems.

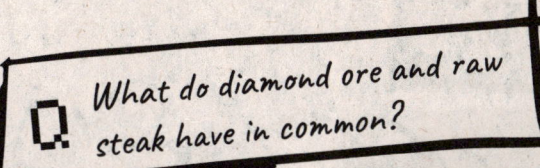

Q: What do diamond ore and raw steak have in common?

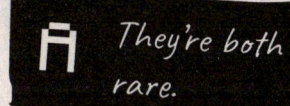

A: They're both rare.

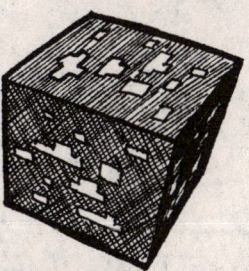

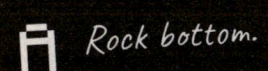

Q: What do you see when you look underneath some ore?

A: Rock bottom.

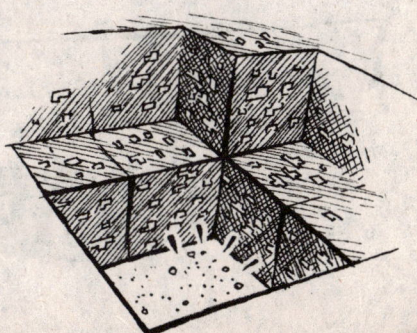

Q Did you hear about the mining accident?

A It was ore-ful.

Steve: Did you hear about the villager that hated coal?

Alex: No.

Steve: Never mined.

Alex: What's your favorite ore? Emerald or lapis lazuli?

Steve: Either ore.

THESE JOKES ROCK!
Put yourself between a rock and a funny place.

Q What did Alex say to the diamond ore?

A I dig you.

Q What did the diamond say to the coal?

A I've been under a lot of pressure recently.

Q What music do ore blocks listen to?

A Rock music.

Q What do you call a man with a shovel?

 **A** Doug.

Q So what do you call him when he's lost it?

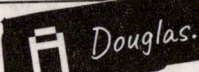 **A** Douglas.

Q Did you hear about the artist who could make anything using shears?

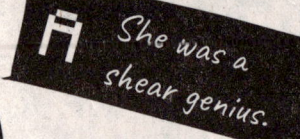 **A** She was a shear genius.

Q What happened when the lumberjack hit the creeper?

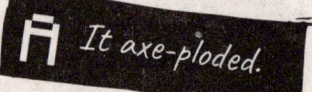 **A** It axe-ploded.

A TOOLBOX OF TITTERS
Let yourself be tickled by these tool jokes.

Q: Did you hear that Alex got hit by a pickaxe?

A: Don't worry, she only suffered miner injuries.

Alex: I've invented the shovel.

Steve: Sounds groundbreaking.

Q What kind of photos do turtles take?

A Shell-fies.

Q What do you do on a turtle's birthday?

A Shell-ebrate!

Two fish were swimming when it started raining. One said to the other, "Quick, get under the bridge. We're going to get wet!"

FISHY FUNNIES

This is dolphin-ately the place for some fin-tastic fish jokes.

Q What party game do fish play?

A Salmon Says.

Q What do you call a fish with no eyes?

A A fsh.

Alex: Do dolphins do things by accident?

Steve: No, they're on porpoise.

Q What's a skeleton's favorite meal?

A Spare ribs.

Q What instrument do skeletons play?

A The trom-bone.

Q How does a skeleton make you laugh?

A It tickles your funny bone.

GRUESOME GAGS
More jokes to really make you scream with laughter!

Q: Why do skeletons hate being high up in the mountains?

A: The cold goes right through them.

Q What do you call a skeleton that stays in the snowy tundra too long?

A A numbskull.

Q Did you hear about the skeleton that broke another skeleton's bow and arrow?

A Now they're arch(er) enemies.

Q Why are skeletons good at telling jokes?

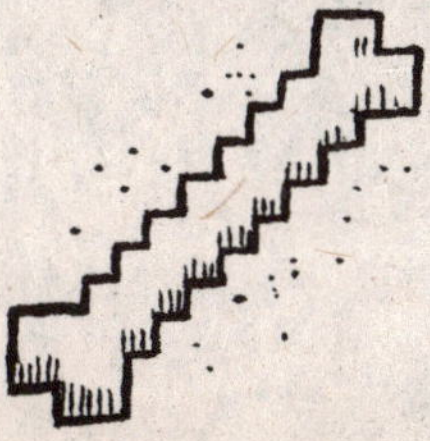

A Because they're so humerus.

TICKLE YOUR FUNNY BONE
These skeleton jokes will hit you in the right spot.

Q: Did you hear about the skeleton that used its bow and arrow in the dark?

A: It didn't know what it was missing.

Q: What do you call a skeleton that can't be bothered to attack?

A: Lazy bones.

Q Why are blacksmiths so interesting?

A They're always riveting.

Q Why are blacksmiths ahead of their time?

A They were shaping metal before it was cool.

Q What do you call someone who steals from the butcher?

A A meatburglar.

JOB JOKES
Who says having a job can't be fun?

Q Why did the cow jump over the moon?

A Steve had cold hands when he was milking it.

Q What do librarians wear on their feet?

A Shhhhhoes.

Q *What kind of horse do you ride at night?*

A *A night-mare.*

Q Did you hear about the mule that had a sore throat?

A It was a little hoarse.

Q Did you hear about the mule that lived next to the horse?

A They were neigh-bors.

HORSING AROUND
We think mule find these jokes a-neigh-zing!

Q Where do you take a sick horse?

A To the horse-pital.

Q What do you call a donkey with 3 legs?

A A wonky.

Q What do you call a donkey with 4 legs?

A Stable.

Q: What did Alex say when she saw the cows on top of the mountain?

A: The steaks have never been higher.

Steve: Did I sleep through dinner?

Alex: Yes, big "missed steak."

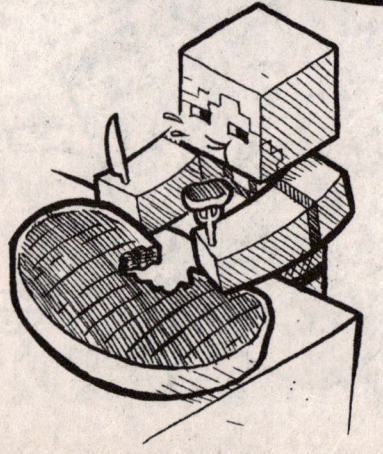
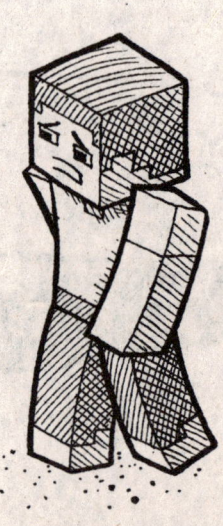

PLEASED TO EAT YOU
Sink your teeth into these meaty morsels.

Q: How do you know when your mutton has gone rotten?

A: It tastes baaaaad!

Q: What do sheep wear to keep their hooves warm in winter?

A: Woolly muttons.

Q: What's a pig's favorite karate move?

A: A pork chop.

Q Why don't llamas like redstone dust up their nose?

A Well, would you like it?

Q: Why does Alex love redstone lamps?

A: Because they light up her life.

RIDICULOUS REDSTONE
A hearty chuckle is just a stone's throw away.

Q What is redstone ore used for?

A Rowing a redstone boat.

Steve: I'd tell you the joke about the redstone circuit, but I'd just be repeating myself.

Q What did Steve say to the sad redstone lamp?

A Lighten up!

JOKE JOURNEY
Let's hope these puns don't go south!

Q Why did Alex sit on the clock?

A She wanted to be on time.

Q Why did Steve take iron and gold in his boat?

A He needed oars.

Q Did you hear about the hungry clock?

A It went back four seconds.

Q What's a zombie's favorite bean?

A A human bean.

Q Why did the zombie go to the doctor?

A It was feeling green.

Q Why did the chicken jockey cross the road?

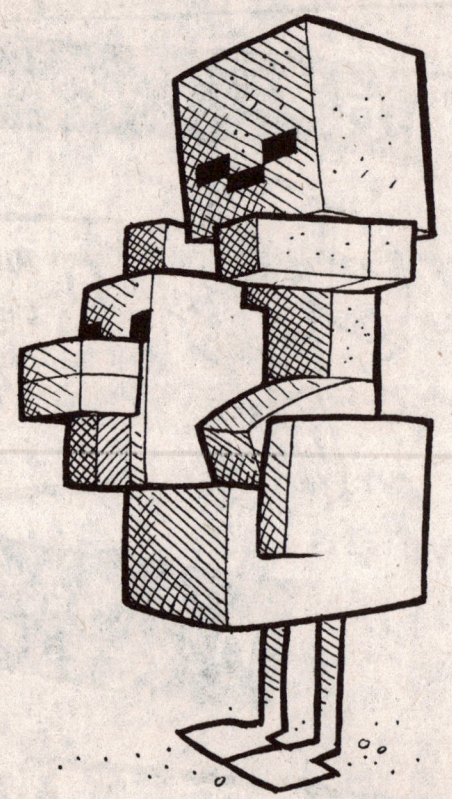

A To get to the other side.

DIE LAUGHING
Don't laugh so much you have to respawn!

Q 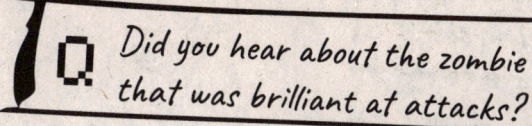 Did you hear about the zombie that was brilliant at attacks?

A 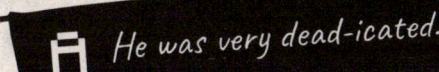 He was very dead-icated.

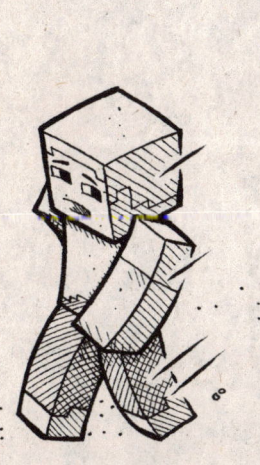

Q 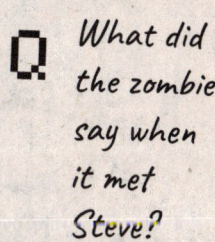 What did the zombie say when it met Steve?

A  Pleased to eat you.

Q What was the baby zombie's favorite toy?

A 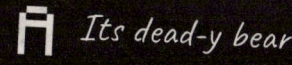 Its dead-y bear.

Q Where should you hide during a zombie attack?

A The living room.

Q Why aren't zombies funny?

A Because all their jokes are rotten.

Q What do zombie farmers grow?

A GRAAAAIIIINNNNSSS!

Q How do you stop a zombie from attacking?

A You block its path.

ZOMBIE ZINGERS

Try not to laugh your head off reading these gruesome gags.

Q Why do zombies sleep all the time?

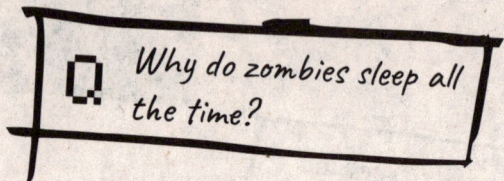

A Because they're dead tired.

Q Why is grass dangerous?

A Because it's full of blades.

Q How many trees did Steve chop down?

A How wood I know?

They really float my boat!

IN THE BEGINNING...

As always, we begin in the Overworld. Get ready to giggle!

Q *How do trees get on the internet?*

A *They log on.*

Q *Did you hear about the mountains that told jokes?*

A *They were "hill areas."*

Do you like the lakes in the Overworld?

MINECRAFT

THE OFFICIAL JOKE BOOK

By Dan Morgan
Illustrated by Joe McLaren

Random House 🏠 New York